For Daina
—PdJ

Miracle *at* St Andrews

JAMES
PATTERSON
& PETER DE JONGE

Miracle *at*
St Andrews

CENTURY

1 3 5 7 9 10 8 6 4 2

Century
20 Vauxhall Bridge Road
London SW1V 2SA

Century is part of the Penguin Random House group of companies
whose addresses can be found at global.penguinrandomhouse.com

Penguin
Random House
UK

This is a work of fiction. All characters and descriptions
of events are the products of the author's imagination and any
resemblance to actual persons is entirely coincidental

First published by Century in 2019

www.penguin.co.uk

A CIP catalogue record for this book is available from the British Library.

ISBN 9781780899947
ISBN 9781780899954 (trade paperback edition)

Printed and bound in Great Britain by Clays Ltd, Elcograf S.p.A.

Penguin Random House is committed to a sustainable future
for our business, our readers and our planet. This book is made
from Forest Stewardship Council® certified paper.

MIX
Paper from
responsible sources
FSC
www.fsc.org   FSC® C018179

1

FOR THE FIFTH TIME on the back nine, my caddy, John Abate, pulls his green military-issue binoculars from the side pouch, and rather than locking in on a target on the 16th hole, the one we're playing, squints into the distance at the leaderboard behind the 9th green.

"Any good news?"

"Afraid not," he says. With his binoculars screwed into his face, Abate could be mistaken for an amateur bird watcher instead of a veteran bag toter on the Senior Tour, albeit one with five days of gray stubble, a diamond earring, and a large New York Yankees logo tattooed on his calf.

"Summerhays is still tied for eleventh at three under," he says, "and Gibson is still two up on you at six under. And they both just parred seventeen."

"You sure about that?"

Abate lowers his binoculars to give me the full benefit of his smirk.

"You don't believe me, look for yourself."

It's late on the final Sunday of the season, and if me and Abate are getting a little testy with each other, it's because we've spent the last four hours of this hot and brutally humid November afternoon fighting for our professional lives. And what makes our predicament all the more frustrating and nerve-wracking and mentally draining is that our fate is largely beyond our control. To keep my card and play another year, it's no longer enough that I play well. Brent Summerhays and Fred Gibson also have to play badly, which is why for the past couple of hours, Abate has spent as much time studying leaderboards as reading greens and pulling clubs. And according to his latest long-distance recon, neither of my colleagues has been doing his part, which means, in all probability, I'm down to my last thirty minutes as a professional golfer.

2

Let me explain.

And please bear with me because it's a little complicated.

To retain your playing privileges in the game of musical chairs known as the Senior Tour, a golfer has to finish in the top thirty-one on the money list, and when me and Johnny A rolled into Sarasota three days ago for the Liberty Mutual Gulf of Mexico Classic, the last full field event of 1999, I was thirty-third on that list. To leapfrog those two places and grab that last spot, two things have to happen. Summerhays, who started the week in thirty-first, has to finish outside the top fifteen, and I have to finish ahead of Gibson, the golfer currently one spot in front of me in thirty-second.

If you're finding it a bit tedious to keep track of all this, imagine how wearying it's been for me tallying up my prize money and checking the standings week after week, round after round, like some junior high school nerd averaging the scores on his algebra tests. But that's the way of the world and vaguely humiliating reality for those trying to hang on to the lower rungs of the Senior Tour, but not so humiliating that I wouldn't sacrifice a digit or two for one more year of it. And with Summerhays and Gibson teeing off on 18, and me and Johnny A a hole and a half behind them on the 16th fairway, we're running out of time and real estate.

Objectively, I know I have no right to complain, not that that's ever stopped me before. As a former advertising copywriter who didn't turn pro until fifty, no one expected me to last twenty minutes out here, let alone four years, but I guess I'm greedy. I'm like that orphan in that musical who has the temerity to hold out his empty bowl of oatmeal and say "Please, sir, I want some more."

To maintain a semblance of dignity, Abate lifts the binocs from around his neck and stuffs them back into the side pouch and we turn what's left of our fragmented attention to the shot at hand. "You got a hundred sixty-five yards to the front edge," says Abate, tossing a pinch of bent Bermuda into the soupy Florida breeze. "A hundred eighty to the pin, wind hurting from the right. And I need to see some focus. We're not out of this yet. So let's keep grinding until the fat lady sings."

Abate hands me the 6, and in a rare display of professionalism I banish the Rubenesque diva from my thoughts and put a good swing on it, holding a high cut against the wind that stops twenty-two feet left of the hole. As usual, my putting stroke is less impressive than my ball striking, and my birdie try scares me and Abate more than the hole. I clean up the remaining four feet for par and we head to 17, still on the wrong side of the bubble, but still alive.

Barely.

3

SEVENTEEN IS A BEAST, a 237-yard par 3 with a bunker right and out of bounds left that's as long and tight as anything we face all year.

"What a nasty hole," I mutter, "even without this wind. We're seniors, for fuck's sake. We're going to be on Social Security and Medicare soon. We're not supposed to play holes like this. It's not good for our cholesterol. And what does it say about a country that it shows such little compassion for its elderly?"

Abate responds to my whining with a blank stare. "You done?" he asks. "You parred it yesterday. You can do it again." He sees no good reason to bring up my bogey on Friday.

The last five holes of Islandside Golf Club run alongside Longboat Key's only major road, Gulf of Mexico Drive, and the Sunday traffic back from the beach has slowed to a crawl. The cars are progressing at the same pace as we are on foot, and after grinding our asses off all day with nothing to show for it, and not knowing if any of it will even matter, it's hard not to see the stalled traffic as a metaphor for our predicament. Certainly, we're as hot and cranky and frustrated as the drivers in their sticky seats.

"And by the way, those frigging horns don't exactly help," I say.

"I can't see how they would," says Abate, who, after countering my negativity all afternoon, is taking a different tack. "Maybe you should walk over and smash a few windshields."

"Might be just what I need. Release the tension. Free me up."

Abate's decision to cut me some slack and let me vent pays instant dividends, and I respond with my best shot in months—a low penetrating 4-wood that never gets more than twenty feet off the ground and holds its line in the wind before stopping just short of the green.

"Golf shot," says Johnny A, doing his best to conceal his surprise. I'm still forty feet from the hole, but they're all uphill so I can give it a good rap, and for the second hole in a row manage a relatively straightforward two-putt par.

"Proud of you," says Abate, and as we stand on the back edge of the green, waiting for our playing partners to finish up, the breeze that fought my 4-wood brings encouraging noise from the gallery up ahead on 18.

First comes an abrupt collective gasp, echoed thirty seconds later by a deep groan. When they are followed soon after by the most pitiable soundtrack in golf (although from our point of view the most uplifting), which is the embarrassed, anemic applause of fans who have just witnessed golfing hara-kiri, Abate and I gape at each other like wide-eyed children.

With the urgency of unexpected hope, he stoops over and yanks at the zipper of the side pouch that holds the binoculars. In the last several hours of overuse, the zipper has lost a third of its teeth, so it requires multiple violent tugs and what feels like twenty minutes before he can rip it open, extricate the field glasses, and refocus them yet again on the leaderboard.

"Talk to me, John. I'm dying here."

Abate doesn't respond, just screws his fists deeper into his eye sockets, and as he digests the latest data on the big board, his mouth stretches into a lascivious grin, so that now he looks less like a bird-watching hobbyist than a demented peeping Tom.

"Actually, you're very much alive. Summerhays and Gibson must have rinsed their second shots on eighteen."

"So what are you saying?"

"I'm saying that Summerhays and Gibson both doubled eighteen. The fat lady has laryngitis. We're back in the hunt."

4

In case you've lost the thread in all this excitement, let me lay out the situation one more time. With their disastrous finishing hole, Summerhays and Gibson, God bless them both, have finally started pulling their weight.

In order to retain my playing privileges for another year and extend my career into the new millennium, the first thing that had to happen was that Summerhays finish outside the top fifteen, and his double bogey on 18 took care of that by dropping him from a tie for eleventh place to sixteenth. The second requirement was that I finish ahead of Gibson, and with his closing double, the two of us are now tied at four under par, so if I can birdie 18, I'll pass him on the leaderboard and keep my card.

Under most circumstances, a birdie on the final hole would be something of a pipe dream, but in this case, it's well within the realm of possibility, because 18 is a short reachable par 5, a birdie hole if ever there was one, and although various issues have crept uninvited into my game and central nervous system in the last four years, I'm still long off the tee. If I can keep my drive in the fairway, I can almost certainly go for the green in two, and if I can land that shot and get down in two putts, Abate and I can party like it's 1999, which it is.

It's amazing what a little calamity from your rivals can do for your worldview. Thanks to Summerhays and Gibson's generous acts of self-destruction, I'm not nearly as cranky and tired as I was moments before. Those honking horns from the poor overheated drivers stuck in bumper-to-bumper traffic sound less abrasive, even celebratory.

For the first time in months, my fate is entirely in my hands. For better or worse, the only person I have to worry about is Travis McKinley, and to emphasize that point, Abate turns putting away the binoculars into an elaborate ceremony. With slow and exaggerated movements, he lifts them over his sweaty head and meticulously winds the strap around them. Then he digs the four plastic caps out of my bag and snaps them over the lenses and eyeholes, as if he is about to put them into storage forever. And then to further emphasize this sense of a new beginning and clean break from everything that has gone before, he takes my perfectly good Titleist and hands me a brand-new one, which has not been subjected to the stress and traumas of the past three hours and reeks of nothing but the box and hope. "We're done grinding," he says. "Time to go birdie hunting."

Part of what makes the 18th at Islandside a great finishing hole is that you can play it two ways. You can play it as a right-angle dogleg by following your drive way with a straight-ahead lay-up, leaving you a short wedge to the green with your third. Or on your second shot, you can bear right over water and go directly for the green, in which case the hole plays harder but shorter. It's a classic risk-reward finishing hole designed to stir up drama.

"The first goal," says Abate, "is not to overswing. On the card, they got it at five hundred fifty yards, but if you cut off the dogleg, it plays closer to five hundred, so we're not looking for anything extra. Your usual swing and yardage is plenty. Don't add a thing. Just put some smooth on it."

Despite the new higher stakes, I do just that, and my low hooking ball flight yields plenty of roll. "Perfect," says John, and for the last time in the season puts the driver back in the bag. "Let's go see what we have left."

Walking as slowly as we can, we head for the ball, which sits in an ideal spot on the left side of the fairway, and after checking his yardage book and pacing off the distance to the nearest sprinkler head, Abate determines we're 248 to the front edge of the green, 266 to the hole.

It's a scary shot, don't get me wrong, but it's a good distance for me—a solid, garden-variety 3-wood, even if the first 200 yards are taken up by a man-made pond, which did in Summerhays and Gibson.

"You're swinging great," says Abate as he hands me the club. "We just need one more." For about twenty seconds, I stand perfectly still behind my ball and imagine with eyes wide open the shot I need to hit, and as I hear the sound of the club face compressing the ball and envision the trajectory as it sails over a row of palms and draws toward the flag, I pat my thigh and feel the metal object in my right pocket.

Although there is no descriptor I love more than "card-carrying member of the PGA Tour," the Senior Tour doesn't actually issue a paper credential. Instead, you get something way cooler—a money clip. To those who've earned one, it's an object of rare beauty, with PGA TOUR inscribed on the front along with their signature logo of a golfer holding his follow-through. And it has a satisfying heft and lovely hinged action. I remember my excitement when it arrived in a little box from PGA headquarters in Ponte Vedra Beach, Florida. That evening at dinner I placed it on the table beside the salt and pepper shakers so we could all admire it and pass it around. For me, the sight and touch of it have never gotten old, and knowing that it's safe and secure in my pocket is a source of comfort.

As soon as I hit it, I know it's enough to clear the hazard. The only question is how close to the hole it will end up. Forgive me for saying this, but I hit it too well, not generally a problem for someone vying for the last secure spot on the Senior Tour money list. Instead of landing just short and bounding up near the pin, it lands hole high and races off the back edge into the little collection area behind the green.

I'm lying two just off the back of a par 5, but when Abate and I see the tight lie and how little room I have to stop the ball on the green, it seems like a miserly reward for such a well-struck shot. Hitting a soft pitch from a tight lie is one of the harder shots in the game, and no one has ever confused me with Phil Mickelson. Maybe that's about to change and I'll have to start wearing a name card, because I catch it just right and hit one of the sweetest little lob shots I can recall.

The same fans who were gasping and groaning minutes ago are oohing and ahhing with appreciation. But when the ball stops rolling, there's still five and a half feet between me and a birdie, sixty-six inches of unfinished business that will determine whether I get to spend a fifth year doing what I love and still do better than all but a handful of people my age on the planet or will be put out to pasture.

"Right edge firm," says Abate, and slaps the polished Titleist into my palm.

My stroke is positive and somehow I resist the urge to peek. So it's just a matter of waiting for the echoing sound of the ball rattling in the cup...but unfortunately, the silence says it all. After a great drive, a bear of a 3-wood, a near-perfect pitch, and a solid putt, I am once again unemployed.

5

ALTHOUGH NOAH IS ONLY in the third grade, the two of us have already honed our early-morning Thanksgiving ritual. While Sarah lingers under the covers and Louie makes do with the rug, we climb the stairs to Elizabeth's old bedroom and pull the two extra leaves from the back of her closet. Careful not to scrape the walls, we carry them downstairs, where Noah scurries beneath the dining room table and undoes the latch. Then, like two epic muscle-bound warriors, we stand at opposite ends and tug until the table groans open and doubles in length.

After we lay in the extra leaves and push it back together, we head to the kitchen and break out the good stuff—the heirloom silver with MCK inscribed on the handles, the crystal glasses, and the fine china. We dig out the small green dishes with trompe l'oeil leaves for Sarah's cucumber salad, the silver gravy boat and the various tureens and serving dishes for stuffing, Brussels sprouts, and the bird itself. Only when the last fork and knife are in their places do we step back and admire our handiwork.

Thank God for Thanksgiving, the pilgrims, and the Indians. In anything but the best of times, the other holidays tend to make you feel like crap, but Thanksgiving actually makes you feel thankful, even a middle-aged ex-pro who just lost his card and is inclined to skew dark and see the crystal as half empty. The two weeks since that missed six-footer in Longboat Key have been pretty shaky. It's great to be home with Sarah, Noah, and the pooch, but I've had my share of anxious moments, both about money—with Noah just halfway through grammar school, there are more than a decade of bills still to arrive—and the question of what, if anything, I am going to do next. If you're one of those people who define themselves by what they do—and who doesn't—the prospect of not doing much of anything is deeply unsettling. As you already know, I'm not much of a putter. Well I'm even less of a putterer, and left to my own devices, it could get ugly fast.

Noah and I have laid out seven settings, and it's going to be wonderful to have the entire two generations of McKinleys gathered around one table. In the last four years, I haven't seen nearly enough of Simon. At the same time that he was going from a good high school soccer player to an elite national junior to the starting goalie at the University of Virginia, the number three ranked team in the country, I was experiencing my own less likely athletic renaissance (that's if you're feeling generous enough to call golf a sport), so the two of us have both spent a lot of time in stadiums and golf courses in different parts of the country. And two weeks ago, he dropped the news that he was bringing a girl, which sent a buzz of anticipation through the household, and when we hear a car in the driveway, Noah and Louie aren't the only ones beside themselves.

They must all have shared a cab from the airport, because when I open the front door our adult children and their girlfriends are standing in the slanting November sun. At least until we hustle them into the vestibule, where for the next few minutes it's every man, woman, child, and dog for himself. At the center of the pawing, flailing, and cooing are Simon, a tall and strapping twenty-one-year-old with thick light brown hair and a lopsided grin, and Jane Anne Lorenzi, an elegant dark-haired woman with porcelain skin. Noah, who sees Simon as his own flesh-and-blood superhero, is clinging to one leg. Beside them in the mosh pit are Elizabeth and her longtime partner and fellow doctor, Sharoz Makarechi. Elizabeth and Sharoz have been an item since med school, and this is Sharoz's fourth Thanksgiving. Sharoz is such an impressive person and lovely, easy company that she won over the remaining McKinleys as profoundly as she did Elizabeth, particularly Louie, who, truth be told, has a bias toward women that is borderline unseemly.

6

ONE OF THE MANY lovely aspects of Thanksgiving is that
the feast is preceded by a cocktail party and the hors
d'oeuvres are as beloved as the big bird. I pour champagne, Noah doles out shrimp cocktail and those little
hot dogs in their baked crust, and we all get our first
good look at Jane Anne. I learn in snippets that Jane Anne
is not an undergraduate but a second-year grad student
working toward a PhD in American studies, and the fact
that Simon has brought home a beautiful doctoral candi-
date at least four years older than himself has the whole
room agog, most of all Elizabeth, the family's reigning in-
tellectual. I'm just happy for him, and as I beam across
the room at Sarah, I can't help but take some small pride
in the fact that Simon has upheld an important McKinley tradition, perhaps the most crucial to our long-term
prospects, which is to fall for women smarter than we are.

When we move to the dining room and my eyes can take everyone in at the same time, my pride in my brood only deepens. With the exception of myself, each and every McKinley is not only happy and thriving, they are coursing with youth and love and beauty, not to mention kicking ass and taking names. So much so, I feel compelled to do something I never do on these occasions—which is make a toast. Reminding myself not to mar the occasion with some off-tone flight of improvisation, I reach for my glass, but before I grab hold of it, Simon has beat me to it and is out of his chair, wineglass in hand.

"I want to say how excited I am that Jane Anne is here and meeting our whole family, all of whom she will soon discover are quite amazing. I also want to let her and everyone else know how happy I am that we are together."

Sarah and I glance at each other in merry amazement. First he brings home this amazing young woman, and now he is delivering formal toasts. What's next?

These days, my thoughts wander backward at the drop of a hat, and as Simon stands over the table, nervous but not the least bit hesitant, it's fifteen years ago and I'm on the sidelines of a scaled-down peewee field in Woodhaven Park for his first game in goal. Simon had already made an impression as a precocious athlete, but what amazed the handful of parents that crisp fall morning was that here was a sixty-pound kid who was prepared to dive at the shoe tops of an onrushing player. In almost every soccer game from peewee to the premiership, there is a gladiatorial moment where an opposing player is rushing in on goal and the goalie comes off his line to meet him. In that instant, the goalie has put everything at risk. Once he leaves the line, he has to get at a piece of the ball or more than likely it will end up in the back of his net. To do that, there can't be an iota of hesitation. All the skill and quickness and speed won't be enough if you're not brave, and Simon has always been brave. I just hope his heart is in good hands.

My mind is still somewhere between that cut-down field and this dining room when Elizabeth raises her glass and clears her throat. "I also want to make a toast," she says, "and share some wonderful news. Sharoz and I . . . are pregnant, or, more specifically, Sharoz is. Five months and counting. We don't know the sex yet and we don't want to know, but we've gotten the results of the amnio and everything looks perfect, so we can't keep it to ourselves any longer."

For what feels like the umpteenth time this afternoon, Sarah and I share a smile and haul aboard this latest development in a lifetime of fascinating twists. Now I have no choice. I don't have the luxury of sitting on the sidelines any longer. If I don't make a toast in the next ten seconds,

I might as well move out, so before I know what I'm doing, I'm finally up and out of my chair.

"First of all, I want to second what Simon said so well
and welcome Jane Anne. Subjecting yourself to all this
McKinley scrutiny is a courageous thing to do, even for
such an accomplished young woman. And we're so glad
you did. So thanks again. And speaking of courage, I also
of course want to salute Sharoz. This is a brave woman.
You have been a part of the family for many years now,
but now you have sealed the deal and become family
forever. I hope you know just how much affection and ad-
miration and love we all have for you, not just Louie. I
also hope that if by chance, you ever decide to have a second child, no pressure, that Elizabeth will do her part as
well."

I look across at Sarah again, and while her eyes are still
merry, this last avoidable quip has evoked more of an eye
roll than a smile. All in all, however, I'm about as happy as
an unemployed fifty-four-year-old can be. If there is any
shadow at all on the proceedings, it's my regret that somehow Simon, the middle child, has been upstaged again.

7

THERE'S NOTHING LIKE DRIVING through the high gates of
a snooty country club and seeing that all three cars in the
parking lot belong to your closest friends. Now that's an
exclusive club. Parked side by side are an '83 Volkswagen
Passat, which at one point was silver, a '77 Buick Riviera whose ambitious restoration stalled decades ago, and
a Honda minivan so nondescript it would make an excellent getaway vehicle. Normally I'm the first to arrive, but
this morning they've all beaten me here, and behind each
car, propped on its stand, is a light carry bag as readily rec-
ognizable as the cars and their owners. As I park, the side
door of the van slides open and I hop into the back row
behind Ron Claiborne (the Passat), Dave Flannery (the
Buick), and Chuck Hall (the man with the van).

Hall, an accountant who played center for Gonzaga,
doesn't have kids. He drives minivans because he likes

them, and they're comfortable and roomy even if you're 6'9". And unlike with SUVs, there's no big-guy macho posturing. All three sip coffee from Styrofoam cups, and Hall fills another from his thermos and hands it back to Flannery, who passes it on to me, but not before Claiborne, the morning anchor for the ABC affiliate, tops it from his silver flask. As always, the flask is filled with Canadian Club whiskey and, according to one of the many traditions of our Friday-after-Thanksgiving round, is referred to as "the best club in Claiborne's bag...by far." Because it is. Then the four of us, who have been friends for thirty years, touch cups and take a hot, bracing gulp.

"I ask you," says Flannery, who has had a long career in marketing, most recently at Abercrombie, "is there a sweeter sound on a cold morning than the chafing of warm Styrofoam?"

"Not in this car," says Hall, timing his comment with a fart.

Says Claiborne, "That's just Chuck's way of saying happy Thanksgiving, Travis. What's new in McKinleyville?"

"You got a couple minutes?"

"I don't think anyone's going to jump in front of us," he says, gesturing at the vacant lot and beyond it the leafless course. I should probably point out that the reason both are empty is because it's twenty-seven degrees and hasn't been above thirty-five in two weeks. Also, that Medinah Country Club—one of the best tracks in America and the site of a PGA Championship and a U.S. Open—is closed, which technically may not apply to us, because none of us are members. We're not fretting the technicalities, because Flannery is related by blood or marriage to half the members of the Chicago Police Department and has a shiny gold shield prominently displayed in his windshield to prove it.

Also, because we are four bad motherfuckers.

"Let me start with the good news. Simon brought a girl to Thanksgiving."

"Wow. Thanksgiving. That's serious."

"Also, Elizabeth and Sharoz are pregnant—five months—sex yet to be determined." This produces a series of grunts and guffaws consistent with three male sapiens of a certain epoch. They sound like a herd of seals sunning themselves on the rocks.

"Is it appropriate to ask who the father is?"

"Probably not. I didn't have the balls to do it."

"Big surprise there." And more sound effects.

"Travis. Please forgive our Neanderthal friends," says Flannery, hoisting his cup again. "They're old, malodorous, and out of touch. *Mazel tov*. So what's the bad news?"

"I lost my card—by one spot and one shot. Or, to

be exact, one six-foot putt which I thought I hit dead center."

"Are we supposed to be surprised that you missed a six-footer?"

"Travis," says Hall from the front row. "We are all aware of the fact that you lost your card. In case you are not aware, we follow your career with some interest and pride via that new development called the Internet."

"I appreciate that. Really. Anyway, enough about me. How are you guys doing?"

"We lost our cards too."

"What do you mean?"

"We all got fired."

"That's hard to believe."

"Downsized, aged out, and fucked over. All in the last three months. And we're hardly an exception. While we were waiting, we could only come up with three people who don't work for themselves or own their company or sit at the very top of the food chain who have managed to stay employed past fifty-five."

"That's awful. So we're all in the same boat."

"No," says Hall, "and that's the point we would like to impress upon you this morning. Unlike us, you can get your job back. And it doesn't require a song and a dance for headhunters or Human Resources."

"If you could get through Q-School the first time," says

Claiborne, "you can do it again. You're twice the player you were four years ago."

"So we are strongly urging, insisting even, that you suck it up, stop whining about six-footers, and get your ass back on tour where you belong."

It's hard to face them. Not only because I know how good they were at what they did, but because I'm the only one who lost his job fair and square. "Thanks for being such good friends. And not just this morning."

"You're welcome.... Now enough of this morbid crap. Let's play golf. No gimmes. No mulligans. No bullshit."

At that, the doors of the van slide open, and four men of a certain age, fortified by affection for the game and each other, as well as by the best club in Claiborne's bag by far, gingerly step into the cold and shoulder their clubs. As we make our way across the empty lot, we look like an older golfing version of the opening credits of *Reservoir Dogs*. Unlike in the movie, however, there's no need to slow down the footage. These days, that's the way we move.

"Any *good* news?" I ask.

"Yeah. Claiborne just got the results from his first colonoscopy. Clean as a whistle.... You know how to whistle, don't you, Ron? You just put your lips together and blow."

8

PEOPLE COMPETE FOR ALL kinds of reasons. Me, it's about making a point and it's always the same one: Don't underestimate me. I may not look like much or have much of a pedigree but I might surprise you. Maybe even kick your ass. In my head, I'm also standing up for my friends and trying to make the same point for them, so that little intervention in the back of the minivan found the mark, and early the next morning, I'm back at Big Oaks driving range on Route 38, third stall from the left, bracing myself for a second trip to Q-School.

For the second day in a row, I was reminded of my good fortune. Not just in what I have been able to do for four years, but how much crap I've been able to avoid. Yes, I'm out of a job at the moment, but unlike my pals and so many of our cohorts, I have a concrete job opportunity. Best of all, mine doesn't require that I rewrite my resume, get a haircut, and invest in a new suit. I don't have to get my teeth whitened and learn how to smile, improve my posture, act younger or more gung ho, or pretend to be anything other than my cranky aging self. I don't have to send out 100 resumes in hope of one response or wade through eight miles of shit to interview for a job that doesn't exist. All I have to do is fly out to Tucson and golf my ball well enough to finish in the top eight. The least I can do is work my ass off in the little time I have to prepare.

At fifty-four, the spirit is willing but the infrastructure is creaky. Wrists, elbows, shoulders, and back require little provocation to balk and can only take so much pounding off these thin rubber mats. My daily quota is 100 balls, one for each of those resumes, and from alignment to setup to contact to follow-through, I bear down on each one. If I catch my attention drifting for even a second, I imagine what it might be like to spend the morning instead in reception in a Chicago skyscraper waiting, along with dozens of other squirming candidates, for a twenty-six-year-old from Human Resources to walk me back to his cubicle. Still, concentrating fully on 100 consecutive swings is harder than it seems, and when I've sent the last range rock out into the gloomy depths, I'm as tired as if I'd played a competitive round.

I stash my clubs in the little closet they've allotted me

by the front desk and repair to the vehicle, where I let the heated seat go to work on my lumbar. I know how lucky I was to get through Q-School the first time around and how difficult it will be to do it again. With 144 players competing for 8 cards, the odds are long, 1 in 18 to be exact. Nevertheless, I probably have a better statistical chance of getting my card back than Ron, Dave, and Chuck have of getting rehired at anything like their old jobs and salaries.

And that doesn't seem right. At a certain point, the world expects you to walk away quietly like an old elephant with sore teeth and disappear. But I'm not feeling cooperative and I guess I never have. I may get locked out but I'm not going to just go away. Not yet.

Fuck 'em.

I think about Elizabeth and the new McKinley in progress in Sharoz's womb and Simon and his new girl and catch myself smiling in the rearview.

How I play out these next few years still matters to a lot of people, from my family to my oldest friends to someone, sex undetermined, who hasn't been born yet. I'm almost doing fifty-five and feel it in every part of me that isn't numb, but I'm persisting. I may be fucked in some ways, but I'm still doing what I like, still attempting something difficult, still focused (for the most part) on the future. If that isn't lucky, what is?

I was going to make the call at home, but I have more privacy in the car. And if I wait that long, I might lose my nerve and not do it at all. The dashboard clock reads 10:23. I set 10:30 as my deadline and the seven minutes fly by with excruciating speed. I might as well be back in ninth grade and staring at the rotary phone on which I will call a girl for the first time. The same feeling as I dial the number and hear the unanswered rings, the same jolt when the ringing stops and a voice cuts through.

"Hey, Dad, what's up?"

"Simon, glad I caught you. Great to see you at Thanksgiving. And wonderful to meet Jane Anne. She's amazing."

"You like her?"

"How could I not? I have a favor to ask. I completely understand if you can't do it because of your schedule, exams, practice, or whatever. But if you could, it would mean a lot to me. Next Wednesday, I'm flying to Tucson for Senior Q-School to see if I can get through one more time. It's a resort course and I know it well. The tour stops there every year and I've played it at least twenty times, including practice rounds. So I'm not looking for local knowledge. What I could use is someone to keep me company and keep my head on straight, so I would really appreciate it if you would consider caddying for me. As I said, I completely understand if you can't. I know you

have a lot on your plate with exams coming up and practice and workouts and now you have this amazing new
girlfriend, but if you could spare a long weekend—"

"Hey, Dad. Stop it. Please. I would love to caddy for
you. Nothing I'd rather do. Just give me the details and
I'll be there.... Hey, Dad, you there...?"

"Yeah, I'm here."

9

No EVENT INSPIRES THE same dread and panic and flop sweat as Q-School, and the senior version is that much worse because it truly is the last train to Clarksville; and sad as it is, many of these golfers have actually been looking forward to getting older and turning fifty just so they can give pro golf one last try. Although someone has to win the tournament, no one arrives in Tucson with dreams of holding up the trophy Sunday afternoon. In fact, winning is the furthest thing from their minds. The only goal is survival, to "get through."

Instead of anticipation or excitement, there's the fear of failure, and it's so palpable it permeates the Omni resort like the smell of mildew after a flood. It makes the corridors feel tighter and longer and the elevators more claustrophobic.

Simon, whom I just picked up at the Tucson airport,

can feel it too, and as he walks through the silent lobby in his gray hoodie, cargo shorts, and sneakers, he flashes a tight smile and says, "I can see why you wanted some company. Everyone is walking on eggshells."

We stay in the room only long enough to drop off Simon's backpack and pull a couple of Coronas from the minibar. Then we take the elevator down to the lobby and slip back outside. To the right is the driving range, and we walk across it to a small elevated area on the far side reserved for the teaching pros, where I happen to know there's a rarely used bench. "Every time I come here," I say, "I make a little pilgrimage to this spot."

The December sun is in free fall, taking with it the afternoon heat, and for the next few minutes we nurse our beers and watch the sky turn orange and purple like a deep bruise. Q-School is a bitch, but the tension of the event and the attendant bad vibes are overshadowed by the profound pleasure of having Simon beside me.

Outside of golf, I've never had much talent for living in real time. It's not till after the fact that I realize the significance of what has just transpired, or what someone was trying to express, and what it might have meant to them or me, but this evening, there's no lag or filter between me and my appreciation.

"Do you remember four years ago when I called home to let everyone know I'd gotten through Q-School?"

"Of course," says Simon.

"I spoke to your mom for a second and she passed me on to you. I was so grateful that you were home because you're the only one who could appreciate what it meant."

"In a house full of brainiacs, we're the only jocks."

"It's true. We're the only ones dumb enough to understand."

"I remember which way I was facing when you told me you had made it and the view from the kitchen window. And I remember about a week later after you got home when you put the money clip on the table for everyone to look at and touch like show-and-tell. That clip was magic. It was like a World Series ring or a heavyweight championship belt."

Fifteen feet from where we're sitting, the grass stops. Until your eyes hit the Santa Rita Mountains, there's nothing but sand and rock, gravel and scrub. The flatness of the vista, interrupted by the occasional cactus, exaggerates the scale of the sky, and the stark line between green and brown reveals the true harshness of the environment and how quickly all this would vanish and the desert return once they turned off the sprinklers.

"So tell me, how did you meet Jane Anne?"

"Last year, on the second day of school, I smiled at her as she walked into the library."

"Eye contact is everything. I really hope they don't make it illegal. The whole world is in a person's eyes. . . . I'm sorry, please continue."

"Over the next few weeks I kept spotting her—by that point I was on the lookout pretty much twenty-four seven—but now the situation was getting critical. You can only smile at a girl so many times. By the third or maybe fourth time, the smiles just start canceling themselves out, until you both realize that's all you're ever going to do."

How does Simon even know this and when did he learn it? It makes me realize how much about him I don't know and never will.

"It's the statue of limitations," I say.

"Dad, I think you mean statute."

"Exactly. *I'm* a statue of limitations. . . . Go on."

"The next time I see her, it's now or never, so I chase after her and ask if she'd like to get a cup of coffee."

"Wow. That makes an eight-footer look like a tap-in."

"She said no. Not only that, she looked at me like I was insane or a stalker."

"That's even more impressive. Anyone can ask someone out who's going to say yes. You approached someone un-approachable. You stormed the barricades. You weren't put off by a little negative feedback."

"Actually, I was. I felt so bad I went back to the dorm

and got under the covers and went to sleep for about three hours. The whole rest of the year, I kept looking for her, but only so I could avoid running into her. This year, first week of school, she comes up to me in the library and asks if the offer to get coffee is still good."

"A year later?"

"Yeah."

"There's that statue of limitations again rearing its ugly head. You were rewarded for being brave. It just took twelve months."

"I said no way. I told her I didn't even drink coffee anymore."

"Bullshit. You drank coffee at Thanksgiving."

"You're right. It is bullshit. I said yes. Not only that, that it was a lifetime offer."

By now the sun has dropped behind the ridge and the last glow of the day barely reaches our bench. Simon taps my arm and nods into the dusk until I spot, some fifty feet away, a coyote slinking across the desert floor, and behind her, three pups struggling to keep up. Although we don't say a word or even move, the mother must sense that her cubs are being scrutinized because she stops in her tracks, turns, and stares at us. Hard. Then she looks back at the pups and continues on her way. Before they blend into the dusk, the mother stops and stares at us again. Then she throws her head back and howls into the sky. Her howl is so high and drawn out and lonesome it makes the hair on my arms stand up.

"That's the best description of Q-School I've ever heard," I say.

10

How to fully convey the four-day freak-out that is Senior Q-School? To give you an idea, Earl Fielder, my best friend out here, survived four tours in Vietnam and said the tournament half reminded him of those bad old days. It had the same sunlit spooky vibe and eerie silence, he said, along with the feeling that something bad was always just about to happen, if not to you then to the guy next to you. And the golfers' superstitions and nervous tics, which got more pronounced as the rounds progressed, reminded him of the way the grunts in his platoon clutched their good-luck charms and tucked pictures of loved ones inside their helmets and prayed to somehow make it home.

Tucson National is a gorgeous track with sparkling green fairways set off by classic TV Western terrain. Tourists from all over the country happily drop $180 to play a round, but for the 144 golfers fighting for those last eight spots, there's nothing lovely about it. All we see are the perils lurking on every hole and the bogeys and doubles lying in ambush, and as hard as it is to stay clear of the bunkers and cacti and man-made ponds, it's harder to avoid the hazards in our heads.

There are no stars teeing it up at Senior Q-School. Legends like Tom Watson, Lanny Wadkins, and Tom Kite are automatically exempt, and except for a sprinkling of journeymen who didn't do enough on the regular tour to rate a free pass, the field is made up mostly of assistant pros and teachers and mini-tour players who for three decades scraped a living at the margins of the game. Despite scant reward, they have ignored wives and reality and hung on to their dreams, even if by any objective measure they ought to have abandoned them twenty years ago. The lack of stars is one reason there are virtually no galleries, little applause, and few witnesses. The other is that the stakes are so high and the odds so long, it makes people uncomfortable to watch.

Which makes me all the more grateful to have Simon on the bag and hear my clubs rattling on his broad back. Despite his comforting presence, I'm tight as a drum, much more than on my maiden voyage to Q-School, because this time around, I know better. My pals weren't blowing smoke. I am a much better golfer than four years ago. I'm also not the same naïve whippersnapper I was at fifty, and from the first tee, I'm fighting myself on every swing and am lucky to get through the front nine two over par.

Because the consequences of a miscue can be career-ending, the pace of play is slower than the lines at the DMV. Every putt is read and reread, every club choice agonized over. When we reach the par 3 tenth and find two groups waiting on the tee, Simon pulls me off to the side and puts his hand on my shoulder.

"Dad, you've got to lighten up. Four years ago, after twenty-five years in an office, you came out here, got your card, and won two tournaments, including the biggest one of them all, the U.S. Senior Open. Your name is on the same trophy as some of the greatest golfers who've ever played. No matter what happens this weekend, you've got nothing left to prove to me or Sarah or Elizabeth or Noah or anyone else."

I disagree with that last part. Until they sit you down and take away your credit cards and car keys, you've always got plenty to prove to yourself and everyone else. But he's got a point and the perspective helps. Thanks to Simon's timely interjection, I go 4 under on the back nine and shoot a 70, good enough to put me inside the magic circle in sixth place. Time will tell if I can keep it up, but it's a start.

11

REMEMBER THAT OLD PUBLIC-SERVICE announcement that showed a big black frying pan on a stovetop and said, "This is drugs," then dropped an egg in the pan and said, "This is your brain on drugs"? Well, I'd love to see what they'd come up with to illustrate a brain under the influence of Senior Q-School. Maybe they'd take a fork and scramble it or leave it in there for six hours—the average length of a Q-School round—until it was so burnt and blackened you couldn't get it off with a jackhammer. Or maybe the actor's hand would shake so badly, he couldn't break the shell. In any case, it wouldn't be pretty.

Pressure messes with a golfer's mind in all kinds of inventive ways, but mostly it makes you think too much. Under stress, the mind tends to get way too involved and chatty, and, like Jack Nicholson's character in *Chinatown*, stick its nose where it doesn't belong. Friday morning, my nerves are still holding up pretty well, maybe because from twenty-five to fifty, I spent my time cranking out headlines and slogans instead of grinding over six-footers. On the front side, I birdie both par 5s and one more on the back, and my 69 inches me one spot up the leaderboard into fifth.

But Saturday afternoon, as we get a little closer to the finish line, the collar tightens and those unwanted voices get darker and cheekier. When they become impossible to ignore, I try to stand up to them and let them know they're wasting their breath. Before every dicey shot, I tip my hat in their direction like an invisible gallery. *I hear you, I see you. I can even smell you. But I'm not going to let you mess with me. And I'm not going to do anything differently no matter what you dredge up.*

For six hours, I'm not just playing the golf course, I'm negotiating and debating with the mob inside my head. Despite the distraction, I somehow maneuver my way around Tucson National one more time, dodge the bulk of the trouble, and avoid the dreaded big number. This time, the best I can manage is even par 72, but because my fellow competitors are contending with similar visitors and voices or worse, it's good enough to climb into fourth and ensconce me a little deeper inside the magic circle.

Still, I know it could all be lost in one bad swing.

12

BY THE TIME WE make it back to our room, Simon and I are burnt to a crisp. And after three nights of room service, we could both use a change of scenery and a different menu.

"I say we get the hell out of here."

"Agreed," says Simon.

"You in the mood for barbecue?"

"Always."

"Then I know a place."

On the road, whenever possible, I stay clear of the big trendy restaurant-bars. My issue isn't the food, although it's usually mediocre and overpriced; it's the god-awful din. The decibel level is so high that by the time I fork over my $40 and stumble out, I feel eroded by noise and can barely remember who I am. In search of peace and quiet as well as sustenance, I seek out smaller, humbler spots owned by individuals rather than corporations or food groups. Often they're ethnic—Thai, Vietnamese, Middle Eastern—and staffed by tight-knit optimistic families of immigrants, but my favorite in Tucson is a distinctly American BBQ joint called Sandy's.

At Sandy's food is served cafeteria style. They lay a piece of wax paper on your tray and drop the sliced meat directly on top. Between us, we order a full slab of center-cut ribs; brisket, marbled rather than lean; and double sides of cucumber salad, mac and cheese, corn bread, and a couple of Yuenglings. Then we carry our trays to a screened-in porch that looks out on a dead-end street, where it's quiet enough to hear the nightlife in the trees.

There are few pleasures more dependable than watching your kid eat, and for a while, I sit back and watch Simon tuck in. At least until I can't resist the urge to interrupt and try to get him to tell me how much he likes it and approves of his old man's taste. "Yeah, it's great," he concedes without looking up.

"You need the calories. You're the one humping the bag."
"True."

As Simon turns his focus to the brisket and sides, I gesture to the corner of the porch. "You see that big guy? That's Howard Twitty, a helluva golfer and a great athlete, and he's leading the tournament. The only reason he is back at Q-School is because his feet let him down. He's had surgeries on both and for years could only practice in sandals. His nickname is the Twitty Bird."

"That's funny," says Simon, but he's not very convincing. "There's something I need to tell you. I was going to wait till after the tournament, but I think you can handle it now."

"Should I be worried?"

"Maybe a little. But it's not like Jane Anne missed her period."

"Good. Because I don't think Elizabeth could handle the competition."

"I've decided to turn pro."

"Really?"

"Yup. MLS teams have been scouting our games all year, and according to my coach, several are interested. Tryouts are in June, and after the season, I'm going to sign with an agent and try to get a contract. Does that sound insane?"

"Simon, you're twenty-one and one of the top college goalies in the country, if not *the* best. I think it would be insane *not* to try to do exactly what you want with your life."

The vehemence of my response takes us both aback. Then makes us laugh.

"Dad, I really appreciate that."

"To insanity," I say, raising my beer.

"To insanity," echoes Simon, raising his own. "And there's something else...."

"You got to be kidding. That's not enough for one tray of BBQ?"

"Not quite. I want you to know that I wouldn't be doing this if you hadn't pulled it off first. Maybe I would have tried to become a coach, but not a player. It wouldn't have seemed possible to me, not for a McKinley from the burbs. Now I want to prove that you weren't a fluke. That I can do it too. So this is your fault, Dad, like it or not."

I know I said that one of the things I appreciate about Sandy's is the acoustics, but now it seems too quiet. Even the cicadas have stopped chirping. For so long, I've felt like the household slacker. Not only because I've contributed less income than Sarah but also because I derived such little pride from what I did. I guess the last four years haven't entirely undone the previous twenty-five, because the idea that anything I might do could affect Simon or Noah in the same way that Sarah's career inspired Elizabeth still seems unthinkable, and it takes a beat or two to register how much that means to me.

"I like it, Simon...."

"Dad, you okay?"

"Yeah."

"You're not going to start blubbering out here in front of the Twitty Bird, are you?"

"Hopefully not."

13

SUNDAY BLOODY SUNDAY. I used to kind of like that U2 song. Now it makes me wince. Since we're tied for fourth, we're in the second-to-last group and not scheduled to go off till 12:53. That gives us a lot of time to kill and too much time to think. I start by administering the best and closest shave I've had in years and savoring every bite of my scrambled eggs as if it's haute cuisine. When we get to the range I try not to hit more balls than usual but extend the time between them, stopping to sniff the air and shoot the breeze between every couple of shots. To my relief I'm hitting it solid and my Big Bertha is really carrying in the warm midday air.

My putting warm-up is less encouraging. Both the pace and the line are vague and the stroke feels squirrelly as hell and after a while Simon steps in and has me practice three- and four-footers so I can at least see the ball going into the hole.

Even after dragging out every part of our routine to within an inch of its life and throwing in a dozen bunker shots from the nastiest lies and stances I can dream up we still have sixty minutes before our tee time, and Simon suggests we head back to the bench we visited our first evening. Because most of the golfers are already on the course and the rest have moved to the putting green, the range is empty enough to safely cross and reclaim our front-row desert seat.

"I wonder how the coyotes are faring," says Simon. "I'm kind of worried about them."

"Me too."

"It's got to be rough out there for a single mom with three mouths to feed. Not as brutal as Q-School, of course, but tough nevertheless."

While Simon surveys the unforgiving landscape, I narrow my focus on the round ahead. I remind myself that it's going to be a struggle. No one gets to traipse through Q-School like it's a walk through the park. Bad things are going to happen and there will be blood—mine, type 0+—and I have to be ready to hang tough and apply a tourniquet when it does. The basic idea is to be prepared for the worst and pleasantly surprised by anything less, and I've been giving myself a version of this preamble with some success since my first peewee tournaments. I'm wrapping things up, getting to the part where I tell myself not just to anticipate a struggle but to embrace it and try in some twisted way to enjoy it, when Simon asks, "Okay if I give her a quick call?"

"Knock yourself out," I say. I wait for him to take out his phone and call his mom or Jane Anne, apprising them of our imminent tee time and offering them one last chance to wish us good luck. Instead he throws back his shaggy head, does something funny with his mouth, and howls into the desert sky. Then he does it again. Simon's calls are still reverberating in the desert air when a third howl, a lot like the first two but even more convincing, comes back.

"Sweet," says Simon, "at least we don't have to worry about her. We can focus on the golf." And although I don't let myself say it aloud, I'm thinking a send-off from a coyote before the last round of Q-School has got to be a good omen. I mean, come on.

Despite the prep work and feral salutations, the last round is a struggle from the moment I plant the first tee in the ground, and surprisingly, considering how it went on the range and the practice green, it's my putter and short game that keep me afloat, not my ball striking.

On the front nine, I don't record a single routine par. Every one is a struggle, a mini-psychodrama. On the first, it takes a breaking downhill nine-footer to save my par and on the second, a thirty-foot chip. Through six holes, my shortest putt for par is five and a half feet, and on 7, when I finally hit a green in regulation, I'm a field goal from the pin. Call me Travis "Houdini" McKinley because I get down in two and on 9 escape the bogeyman again, this time from a fried-egg lie in a greenside bunker.

My scorecard—nine straight pars for a 36—should come with an asterisk and a five-page footnote. And when I walk off the 9th and nearly trip on a blade of grass, I realize how much all that grinding has taken out of me. Holes like those are like dog years. Each one is the equivalent of three or four, and although I'm only halfway home, I feel like I've already played thirty-six.

Actually, I'm a lot less than halfway home, because the next nine are going to require that much more. When Simon and I take the gravel path that snakes through the desert to 10, it feels like we've crossed the border into a different country. In this new realm, aka back nine on Sunday, the air is thinner and the light warped and the most rudimentary aspects of the game—swinging with rhythm, taking the putter back smoothly, following through—require inordinate concentration.

On 10, I sink another six-footer for par, but there is only so much pressure a fifty-four-year-old central nervous system can withstand before it springs a leak. On 12, I lip out a four-footer for par, and on 13 and 15, fail to get up a down. After three bogeys in four holes, I feel like a retiree dipping into his IRA way too soon. The precious hard-earned birdies I spent three days hoarding are flying south for the winter at an alarming rate, and with a sickening feeling of inevitability, I'm slipping down the leaderboard from fourth...to fifth...to sixth, and, after an excruciating three-putt on 17...to seventh. Now I'm hanging on to my card by my fingertips and my momentum is all in the wrong direction. Forty lousy minutes have undone three days of hard work and my margin of error is down to one stroke.

Don't act like this is some kind of surprise, I tell myself. *You knew a test was coming, so let's see what you can do. Q-School is officially in session.*

14

SIMON AND I CLIMB onto the last tee box and squint into the late-afternoon glare. To our left is the Sonoran Desert and to the right a much smaller man-made facsimile in the form of a long deep bunker. Between them a narrow fairway doglegs right and slightly uphill to an undulating green 420 yards away.

"Everything that's happened in the last four days is ancient history," says Simon. "Everything that's happened in the last hours is medieval history. The tournament starts now. Let's be clear on how we want to play it."

The 18th at Tucson National is a perfectly adequate finishing hole, but nothing to write home about, and bear in mind I don't need to bring it to its knees, earn its respect, or even get its attention. For the pearly gates of the Senior Tour to creak open one more time, all I have to do is slink off with a bogey, something half of you could do with a little luck. But if you play this cursed game for a living and understand the innate perversity of the golfing brain, you know that sometimes, when you absolutely need one, a bogey can be harder to attain than a par or even a birdie.

Among pros and high-stakes hustlers, there are two schools of thought on how to play a 4 when all you need is a 5. The first says play it start to finish as a 5. Leave that corny head cover on the driver and tee off with a 7-iron that leaves you well short of the trouble. Then hit another 7 well short of the green, then wedge it on in three, two-putt, and walk away quietly. As its adherents put it, "golf is not a game for heroes."

Option #2 is to play for par and even birdie, and if necessary settle for a bogey. Followers of this point of view concede that heroism is overrated but that's no reason to be a pussy. Besides, playing too safely can often be hazardous to your health. Play for a 5, they say, and realistically that's the best you can hope to score, and if anything goes awry, say a botched wedge or three-jack from thirty feet, all you've done is outsmart yourself. Because it feels more positive and still leaves you that extra stroke in your back pocket, I've always leaned toward the second option, but then again, I may be back at Q-School for a reason.

"What do you think?" asks Simon.

"I like driver," I say.

"Me too," says Simon. "You hit driver the first three rounds and made par every time. Even with the tees back today, it's only two-oh-seven to carry that bunker and you've been carrying it two-sixty all day. All we need is one more decent swing."

Simon hands me the driver and as I did the first three days, I aim just right of the bunker and play for my draw to pull it back to the middle, or ideally to the left side of the fairway for a better line to the green. Maybe it's those four bogeys in the last eight holes, or that little voice that waits till the very top of my backswing to inquire as to why I'm not playing the 7-iron, or maybe the simple fact that I'm choking my brains out, but I don't put nearly as good a swing on the ball Sunday afternoon as I did Thursday, Friday, and Saturday. Funny how that happens, and instead of gently curling in at about 235 yards, it hangs a sharp left at 195.

"Please," I whisper, "carry that gorgeous bunker."

Despite my smarminess, the ball dives into the sand, and when it clings to the bank just short of the lip, I utter an even more desperate follow-up.

"Don't plug! For God's sake!"

Whether it's the power of prayer or gravity, my Titleist topples from its little self-made indentation and trickles down the slope. Now my concern is that it roll far enough, but since two prayers for one shot is pushing it already, I hang on to what's left of my dignity and Simon and I hustle to the bunker to find out exactly what we've got.

15

WHAT WE'VE GOT IS a situation. The good news is the lie is perfect, not surprising considering the ball has just rolled half a dozen feet. And according to Simon's yardage book, we're only 157 from the front edge. The less good news is the lip. It's high and fat and looming and as they whisper ominously in the broadcast tower, it's definitely a factor.

But how much of a factor? To reach the front of the green, I need a 7-iron, and the 7 should give me the loft I need to clear the lip. As long as I catch it right. I remind myself it's not too late to retreat to option #1, golf is not a game for heroes, etc., wedge it out of the bunker and then wedge it onto the green in three, but for the same reason I was reluctant to tee off with the 7, I'm not disposed to hit the wedge now, not when a well-struck mid-iron will put me on the dance floor in two and give me the luxury of three-putting for my card.

Simon pulls the 7, and I descend into my adult sandbox.

From behind the ball I pick a target twenty feet left of the flag and picture the ball comfortably clearing the lip and arcing toward the green, but as I take my stance and hover the club face above the sand, the demons of Q-School must smell blood, because they are circling overhead like buzzards and flapping their furry wings. I block them out as best I can and remind myself I don't have to hit it perfect, but under no circumstances can I catch it thin. My miss has got to be on the fat side. To err toward fatness, I dig my feet into the sand a titch deeper and choke up on my 7-iron a fraction less.

My last thoughts before my waggle are reasonable and generic—*keep your feet quiet, swing within yourself, and maintain your balance*—but when you add the crucial earlier exhortation to if anything hit it fat, that's a compendium of swing thoughts, and as soon as I make contact, I know I did precisely what I told myself I mustn't do. The shot I envisioned does not come to pass. Instead, the click of club face and ball is followed almost instantly by the thud of ball striking turf.

Rather than bounding forward some piddling distance, the ball rockets straight up into the Arizona sky like Old Faithful, or maybe more like a towering spring training pop-up. As it reaches its apex, I note the disconcerting fact that it is directly over my head where the buzzards used to be, and when it begins its descent, my heart plummets with it and the panic in my chest congeals into nausea when I realize that if I don't move, the ball will hit me, and if that happens it's a two-stroke penalty, I'm lying four in the bunker, and whether the ball actually kills me or not, you might as well take me off the respirator, because I'm as good as dead.

As the ball drops, I scramble to get out of its way, but I can't get any traction. In my desperation to reach higher ground, my FootJoys struggle for purchase and then give way and slide out from under me. With my eyes locked on the ball, which is still bearing down on me with what feels like highly personal and malevolent intent, I fall straight back, and as I do I lose sight of the ball in the blinding sun.

16

My vertiginous fall sends me reeling backward in time as well as space, and the days and months and years spool past in a furious blur. When the footage skids to a halt, I'm on another golf course on another Sunday afternoon and I'm seven years old, playing in my third peewee event on a par-3 course in Kankakee, Illinois. After seventeen holes, me and Richie Makepeace, my archrival, are all square, and I guess I've been fighting a hook under pressure since the beginning, because my drive has nestled into the thick rough left of the 18th fairway just short of a large tree.

My predicament in Illinois was not all that different from the one I just faced in Tucson. Except that rather than having to get the ball up quickly over a lip, I needed to keep it down and under the limb of a knotty pine.

Even at seven, I knew enough to position the ball back in my stance, but despite my best efforts, the ball popped up on me, clipped the underside of the branch, bounced hard right into the trunk, and caromed straight back at me so quickly I barely had time to duck out of the way. And when I turned to see where the ball had landed, I inadvertently stepped on it.

As freakish bad breaks go, it was right up there with this one, but forty-seven years would have been enough to put it behind me forever if not for what I did next, or didn't do, which was assess myself a two-stroke penalty, take off my cap, concede the hole and the match, and shake Richie's hand. Then wait until I was safely in my mother's car to start bawling. Instead, I looked over my shoulder, saw that Richie hadn't noticed, and played on.

Yeah, I was only seven, and you'd be hard pressed to find anyone on tour who as a junior never succumbed at least once to that same temptation, but that didn't make it any better. I cheated plain and simple and the worst part is I went on to "win" the tournament. It got a certain amount of attention—photograph in the local paper, congratulations from friends and relatives, and it was the emptiest feeling, far worse than losing, and hung over me the rest of that summer. From that moment on, I was cured and never considered cheating again, not because that one incident turned me forever into an upstanding young man, but because it felt so crappy, and wasn't the whole point of practicing and getting decent at something to feel good about yourself?

17

"DON'T MOVE," SAYS SIMON.

Simon's voice brings me back to the present, but the loss of balance, blinding light, and jarring impact, not to mention the intergalactic time travel, disoriented me sufficiently that it takes a few seconds to realize that I've been delivered back not to a beach, but to Tucson. Only after I've connected a few additional dots do I realize that I'm in a fairway bunker, which is on the 18th hole of Tucson National Golf Course, and that it's the final hole and round of Q-School. Oh, yeah, and I'm flat on my back.

As instructed, I lie frozen in the sand, little black circles floating in my eyes until they readjust to the light. When I finally turn my head, I'm staring eyeball to ball at the black script logo of my Titleist 3, which rests in a perfect lie on top of the sand two inches below my outstretched arm. It's great to see my ball again but the crucial question is "What do I lie?"

Very carefully, so as not to touch it or cause it to move, I lift my arm and roll away from the ball and onto my stomach and then up to my knees. Then Simon pulls me out and brushes off the sand and squeezes my shoulder. "You all right?"

"That depends. Did the ball hit me?"

"No."

"You sure?"

"It was very close but I didn't see or hear anything. Did you?"

"No."

"Did you feel anything?"

"No."

"Then we dodged a bullet and we're still in the hole. Take care of this next shot and we can get out of here in one piece."

Adding to my good fortune, the ball is now at least a yard farther back in the trap, which makes the lip less of an issue, and considering all my gyrations and flailing, the lie is a minor miracle. Although I'm still a bit wobbly, my 7-iron clears the lip with room to spare and rolls onto the front edge twenty-two feet below the ball. It's the perfect leave, straight and uphill. Even in my discombobulated state, I know I can two-putt from there, and I do, but rather than relief and elation, all I feel is the red-hot shame from forty-seven summers ago.

"Dad, you just got your card back. What's the matter?"

"It's that lie in the bunker. It was just too good. On a ball coming straight down from that height, the ball should have plugged or buried, but it was sitting up like someone had placed it there. I don't see how that could have happened if I hadn't broken its fall."

"Dad, the ball didn't hit you. You would have felt it."

"Probably, but between the fall and sun and impact" — I don't mention my round-trip flight to Memory Lane — "a second or two are unaccounted for. Plus, my shirt came untucked as I fell so the ball could have hit my shirt without me feeling it."

"The ball didn't hit you."

"Maybe not, but you're not completely sure of that, and neither am I."

What I didn't do forty-seven years ago as a seven-year-old marred what should have been a wonderful carefree summer. I'm not going to get melodramatic and say it robbed me of my youth, but you get the idea. If I get this wrong as an adult, it could cast a shadow over the rest of my days, and between Simon's potential pro career, Sharoz and Elizabeth's biscuit in the oven, Noah's decade

or so left at home, and what I hope will be another wonderful quarter century or more with Sarah, I have way too
much to look forward to to risk that.

"Simon, I got to take a seven."

"Suit yourself, old man."

18

SIMON'S FLIGHT FOR CHARLOTTE leaves in less than two hours, which is probably just as well, because it gives us less time to dwell on my debacle in the bunker, which Simon is taking even harder than me. After I sign for my card and pick up my check for my twelfth-place finish, we hurry to the car, where Simon's backpack is waiting in the trunk, and head to Tucson International.

"Dad, I still can't believe you did that."

"It was the lie. It was too good. There's just no other explanation for it."

"It's called *luck,* Dad. You got lucky. The universe smiled on your sorry ass down there in the bunker and threw you a bone. And instead of saying *thank you very much, I really appreciate that,* you threw it back."

"Listen, maybe you're right, but overall, when it comes to the important things, I know just how lucky I am, and

I wasn't prepared to mess with that for two strokes on a scorecard. It may sound weird but I am okay with everything that happened this weekend, good and bad. A lot of that has to do with you. What you told me at the restaurant last night means more to me than getting my card. Besides, being a pro athlete is not all trophies and good times. There's a lot of heartache, too. So maybe it's good that you got a taste of that as well."

"A lot more than a taste. It was a bellyful. I'm just glad I don't play a sport where you're expected to call phantom penalties on yourself. In soccer, you do anything you can get away with, including diving in the penalty box."

"It wouldn't work in golf. It's spread over too many acres. There's no way to keep an eye on everyone."

"Maybe not," says Simon. "But that was bullshit."

"Well, if I didn't survive Q-School, at least the coyotes did. That's something, right?"

"I suppose."

"And speaking of your career for a minute, it's not going to be easy, Simon. Thousands of people from all over the world will be competing for every spot, and except for the occasional freak of nature, everyone's pretty even, talent-wise, so you're going to have to be prepared to fight and claw for everything." Hearing even an approximation of Lombardi-speak coming out of my mouth is disconcerting, but being a role model is a little like being the best man at a wedding. You have to rise to the occasion, even if you're not exactly a natural.

For the rest of the drive, neither of us says a word. Despite what happened on 18, it's a peaceful quiet, the kind when people are comfortable enough with each other that they don't feel the need to fill the silence. The traffic is light and the signs for the airport arrive too soon, and as I pull up in front of the departures terminal, I miss Simon already. I hop out first and reach into the trunk and fumble in the dark for his backpack.

"I'm proud of you, Dad," says Simon with a gentle smirk. "I could have gone for a different ending, but the weekend meant a lot to me, too. And hopefully, I learned something." Then he gives me a long hug, shoulders his bag, and heads for the terminal.

As he pushes through the revolving door, I tap my empty right pocket and smile. The check for $4,533.33, the payout for twelfth place, is no longer there. It's in the side pocket of Simon's backpack and endorsed to him. Along with it is a short note scribbled on an envelope in the scorers' tent after signing for my 77. I might not have it exactly right, word for word, but this is close:

Dear Simon,

I can't tell you how much it meant having you on the bag this weekend. The money, which we won together, is my way of saying thanks and investing in your career. I want you to use it to hire a trainer so that when you go to tryouts in five months, you'll be in the best shape of your life. Professional soccer is not some quasi-game/skill like golf. It's the real deal and it's dangerous, most of all for the goalie. Being stronger and faster and more flexible won't just make you better, it will keep you safer. So do some research, find the best trainer in the area, and get to work. If you're reading this, I guess you've already found your new money clip, too. That it's in your hands makes me very happy. It's your turn now.

Love you,
Your old man
Tucson, 12/7/99

P.S. Please feel free to spend some of the money on Jane Anne.

19

THROUGH THE TALL GLASS windows of the terminal, I watch Simon from behind as he walks up to the Eastern Air Lines counter, picks up his boarding pass, and hustles toward his gate. Unlike him, I'm in no rush. My flight to O'Hare isn't till morning and for a few minutes—ten, fifteen, maybe more—I sit at the curb with the engine running and sift through the wreckage.

Instead of reliving the catastrophe on 18 and the botched holes and lousy swings that made the difference between twelfth and eighth, I return to last night's dinner at Sandy's, where after wiping the barbecue sauce from his mouth, Simon told me he was turning pro. Rather than tormenting myself about this or that putt that didn't drop or the dubious thinking down the stretch, I focus on the pleasure I got from turning over the prize money to Simon. Golf figures less in the replay than my recollections of working side by side for four days. And some of my fondest recollections are the least eventful—eating meals together, sitting on our hotel beds catching the highlights on ESPN, enjoying each other's company and bad jokes, and simply sharing time.

When I finally pull away from the curb, the sun has set and the sky is streaked with orange. Driving as slowly as the white-haired men and blue-haired women who have just dropped off or picked up their grandchildren, I slip into the easy Sunday-evening procession back to-ward town. The road that leads to the freeway is lined with small strip malls whose modest businesses are closed for the evening. The only light comes from gas stations, low-budget motels, and the occasional billboard.

I'm heading with little enthusiasm in the direction of the hotel when a brightly colored food truck catches my eye, along with the impressive line of people waiting to order. Grateful for an option other than room service or a loud antiseptic restaurant, I switch lanes and turn into a dim parking lot sprinkled with beat-up old cars and pickups. The people in line are all men, and based on their sweat-stained shirts and hats, they've had a harder and longer workday than me. The fragments of overheard conversation are in Spanish.

As I'm waiting in line, my cell goes off in my pocket, and although I don't recognize the number, I answer it.

"Travis, this is Bob Herbert. I cover golf for the *Tucson Gazette,* the morning daily out here. Got a minute?"

"Sure."

"I heard about what you did on eighteen and taking a seven. Can you take me through that decision?"

"It was pretty simple. I wasn't sure if the ball hit me and I'm still not. So I had no choice."

"Part of the reason I'm asking is that there was a cameraman shooting color for KXP News and he happened to film your shot out of the bunker."

"And?"

"I'm calling from their editing truck. We just went through the sequence frame by frame and it clearly showed that the ball never hit you or any part of your clothing."

"You're absolutely sure about that?"

"One hundred percent."

Rather than respond, I gaze above the truck at the orange-streaked sky.

"Travis, I know this has to be upsetting, but can you share your reaction to this news?"

"So be it."

"That's it?"

"That's it," I repeat, but what I'm thinking is that after forty-seven years, me and Richie are finally all square. "And thanks for the call. I was going to find out sooner or later and I'd just as soon find out now."

I order two quesadillas and a Tecate and hunker down on the curb. The orange has drained from the sky and a dramatic sunset has eased into a chilly desert night, and although the seating is a tad harsh for a bony middle-aged butt, I feel entirely at ease and the food is delicious. If by some miracle I ever make it back to the tour and Tucson, I'll keep an eye peeled for a red and green truck emblazoned with AQUI CON EL NENE ("here with the baby") in fat blue script.

20

THE BEER DONE, I pull myself off the curb, discard the trash, and walk contentedly toward my car, noticing on the way that one business in the strip mall is open—a little tattoo parlor called The Painted Lady.

I'm still in no hurry to return to my hotel. The lobby, filled with dazed and damaged golfers of a certain age, will be no picnic, and despite not getting my card, I'm not feeling the same gloom. I know I should feel like the unluckiest golfer on the planet right now but if anything, I'm feeling oddly celebratory. And instead of getting right back on the road, I leave the key in my pocket, roll down the windows, and inhale the cool desert air.

Tattoo-wise, I'm a fifty-four-year-old virgin and expect to die that way, but as I linger in the parking lot, I consider what, if I were to get one, I might engrave on my skin. I suppose I could get a drawing of Louie, a simple rendering of his distinctive terrier outline. Seeing it would always make me smile, but it seems wrong to honor a pet, however worthy, while he's still going strong.

Warming to the assignment, I consider a tattoo suggestive of Tucson and the desert, like a cactus or a wily coyote. As images, I like both, and you could argue that a prickly cactus captures my personality, but they are too ambitious, i.e., painful, to consider even hypothetically. And although the weekend was positive in important ways, do I really want to be reminded every day for the rest of my life of Q-School 2.0? I don't think so.

Better to get something directed toward the future. Perhaps I could come up with some eloquent message to self that would exhort me in an appropriately low-key way to carry on and persist in my pledge to myself and my old friends to claw my way back onto the tour. Anything that would help me overcome these recent setbacks and ensure that I don't turn into one more premature retiree is worth considering.

Three candidates present themselves. The first is *It takes a lot of heart to play this game.* That's something Earl told me my rookie season, and after four years on tour and four days in the desert, I can vouch for its veracity. I also like the fact that it applies to this short life of ours in general and not just golf, which to be honest, I'm pretty sick of at the moment. Then comes a phrase my mother often said to me, *O ye of little faith,* which is another version of the same message, a reminder to believe in myself and resist the inclination to go dark. I also like the simplicity and directness of my mantra at the driving range, *Don't go away.*

I don't know what you think, but my favorite is the pithy *Don't go away.* I like it so much that without actually deciding to do so, I find myself rolling up the windows, locking the car, and walking toward The Painted Lady, although walking, which suggests free will, is misleading. It's more like I'm standing on a conveyor belt that is pulling me toward the neon sign.

As I get close enough to read the OPEN sign dangling on the door, it dawns on me that what I am doing is crazy and impulsive and permanent, the perfect cocktail for regret, but I can't seem to stop the conveyor belt and soon my hand is twisting the knob and I'm stepping across the threshold.

The place is small and narrow and tidy. Sitting behind the counter is a pretty gray-haired woman with glasses reading the *Tucson Gazette.* She is wearing a sleeveless T-shirt and her elegant shoulders are covered with elaborate designs. For some reason the fact that she is reading a newspaper is comforting.

"Can I help you?" she asks, folding the paper in her lap.

"I'd like to get a tattoo."

"I thought you might say that." She has a lovely smile. "Have you had one before?"

"Nope."

"Have you been drinking?"

"One Tecate to wash down my quesadillas."

"Aqui con el Nene?"

"Yup."

"Place is great, isn't it?"

"The best."

"So you were in the neighborhood and figured you'd drop in and get a tattoo?"

"Basically."

"What do you have in mind?"

"Just a very simple inscription in simple type on my left forearm."

"What's it going to say?"

"Sarah."

21

OUTSIDE THE KITCHEN WINDOW a dusting of snow clings to the bird feeder and bare branches. The first storm of the winter turned out to be an overhyped bust, but it was enough to cancel hundreds of flights in and out of the Midwest. By the time I'm back in my kitchen with Sarah and Louie, it's after midnight. Louie pants at my feet, still recovering from his celebration at the front door, and Sarah looks pretty glad to see me too. "Noah stayed up as late as he could," she says, and pours us both a glass of red. "You okay?"

"Yeah."

"Truly? After what happened on Sunday and spending all of today at the airport? I was afraid Louie and I were going to have to put you back together piece by piece like a jigsaw puzzle."

"I had a great time with Simon, and that helped a lot.

Not to mention the fact that I get to return to my wonderful wife and pooch. Despite what did or didn't happen on eighteen, I'm counting my blessings. And I have major news. Simon is turning pro."

"I wonder where he got that idea from.... God, I think I just made you blush."

"It's kind of weird. I never saw myself as a role model."

"You're a good role model, Travis."

"You really mean that?"

"Of course I do.... What's that on your arm?"

"Oh, that? A little something I picked up in the desert."

"I have some cortisone cream in the cabinet."

"I'm afraid it's more serious than that."

"A bite from a tarantula? Or a venomous snake?"

"Even worse. I got bit by you." I extend my arm.

"...Travis...I can't believe you did that. Are you having a midlife crisis?...Again?"

"Probably. But I'm on top of it."

Sarah leans toward me and kisses me. Then she gets out of her chair and joins me on mine. "I have a better idea," she whispers. "Why don't *I* get on top of it?"

22

I'M TRYING TO GET off to a strong start but the way the morning sun catches my computer screen is distracting in the extreme. Reluctantly, I push back from my desk and lower the shades. That takes care of the glare but leaves the room dark and dreary, so I return to the window and raise the shades several inches. When that feels too bright again, I split the difference... then lower them a quarter of an inch more... and then another... and then raise them a sliver.

In the process of all this fine-tuning, I can't help but notice that my computer screen is filthy. If it weren't so egregious I'd ignore it and plod on, but it looks like it hasn't been cleaned for years. In the back of a drawer, I find a never-opened container of iKlear Apple Polish. I spray some onto a shammy and wipe down the screen quadrant by quadrant until every last smudge, streak, and fingerprint has been eliminated.

What a difference! Now the computer screen sparkles and the scent of cleaning agent hangs in the air. At first, I find it pleasant and bracing, but rather than fading, it grows stronger and more pronounced and maybe even toxic, until in its own way it's as distracting as the glare or the dust. I crack the windows, then put on a sweater against the chill and get back to work. The sweater is plenty warm. Too warm, maybe, and bulky and cumbersome. I feel like I can barely move my arms. A thinner sweater is not warm enough and a third itchy so I go back to the thin one and wear a blazer over it. Perfect.

Did I mention I'm writing a book? Sarah's reaction to my tattoo was more than I had hoped for, and Noah thinks it's kind of cool too, but the problem with tattoos is that it's hard to build a life around them and they don't solve the problem of what to do all day. After reviewing my options, I decided to write a memoir about the rags-to-riches-to . . . sweaters . . . story of my career as a pro golfer.

I know I have some decent material and, after spending twenty-five years in advertising, some experience as a writer, but I underestimated just how difficult it would be to get the working conditions right. Either it's too bright or dim, there's too much glare or shadow, it's too breezy or stuffy, and every day it's different. And although I rarely get any, I find it very difficult not to keep checking my email or what's happening on the Senior Tour without me, sometimes following Earl and Stump hole by hole. After two weeks of work, I don't have much more than a title—*Making the Cut and Missing It: The Journey of a Journeyman*—and to be honest I had that the first day.

When the lighting, temperature, and wardrobe issues have been sorted, it's almost eleven. Not quite time for lunch but I should probably take Louie for his walk. He's been a little sluggish lately and the fresh air would do him good. Reluctantly, I push away from my desk again. Louie lies on his side on the carpet in a warm circle of sun and I jangle the leash in front of his nose. Normally that's all it takes, but this time Louie refuses to be roused, perhaps because he's already been on three walks this morning.

"Louie, don't make me beg," I say, and shake his leash again, but Louie doesn't so much as blink. "Okay, fine, I'm begging."

23

"HAVE YOU EVER GIVEN any thought to television?" asks Ditkoff.

"As a matter of fact, I've been thinking about those new flat-screens."

"I'm not talking about purchasing a television, Travis." Ditkoff wears a bespoke suit, gleaming tortoiseshell glasses, and, on his arthritic claw of a hand, a Rolex Daytona. While none of those distract from his age, they combine to offset it, so that at eighty-six he is simultaneously stooped, shriveled, and undiminished. Not that I am in any position to be ageist. "I meant being *on* television."

"I've been on television already, Bob. It didn't work out too well."

"If you're referring to McKinley vs. Peters at the Ding Dong Lounge in Honolulu last year, I beg to differ. That little skirmish put you in the conversation, my friend. Introduced you as a colorful and outsized media character. A man's man. A bro's bro. Now it's my turn to step into the ring and help you monetize that."

It's 7:15 a.m., and me and the most powerful agent in television news are sharing a window table in the Signature Room on the ninety-fifth floor of the Hancock building. I guess I've lived a sheltered life, because this is my first power breakfast. Till now, my breakfasts have been strictly nutritional. If I'm having a little trouble focusing on Ditkoff's pitch, it's due in part to the spire of the Sears Tower blinking over his left shoulder and the endless view of Lake Michigan over the other. Then there's the spectacle of Ditkoff himself.

On my plate are eggs Benedict, which I assume based on the price have been perfectly prepared, and at every table, lawyers and investment bankers are forming and breaking alliances, hatching and scuttling schemes, placing and hedging bets. By 7:45 a.m. the energy is electric, a little like the putting green before the last round of a big tournament.

"Your win at the Senior Open at Pebble gives you the bona fides," says Ditkoff, "and as a former copywriter you can presumably turn a phrase, and the brawl in Honolulu established you as a regular guy. Put it all together and it spells money. If my instincts are right, and they are, you could soon be far better known and compensated for what you do with a microphone in your hand than any-thing you did with a golf club. No disrespect."

It's all a bit overwhelming, and when I'm slow on the uptake, Ditkoff is more than ready to pick up the slack. "I've got juice at CBS," he says, "a lot of juice," and as if to emphasize the point takes a sip from his own enormous glass of juice—half cranberry, half pomegranate, splash of prune. Over the next ten minutes he drops the first names of his clients, and it's only through context and repetition that I come to realize that "Danny," whom he has represented for twenty-eight years, is Dan Rather, and "Jimmy" is Jim Nantz, the purring baritone of the Masters. "CBS dominates golf, and I've got half the ponies in their stable. You want a six-week tryout, all I have to do is pick up the phone."

Ditkoff is on my side. He is offering to be my mentor and guide, my agent and benefactor, and a person could not have a more powerful and persuasive and life-changing ally than Bobby Ditkoff. So why do I feel like I just got mugged in broad daylight?

"Bob, I'm very flattered and grateful that you reached out. Still, it's a lot to digest and I need to talk it over with my wife and young son, who is still in the third grade. Plus, I just started working on a book."

"That's great. Once you get your face on TV, someone might actually want to buy it. How's that going?"

"It's only been a few weeks, but I already have a pretty good outline and title."

"That bad, huh? Travis, I get it. You've been on the road for four years and you just got home. By all means, take as much time as you need. Think it over carefully, discuss with your wife and son. Then call me tomorrow morning."

24

"THIS WEEK," SAYS BURT Kearns, "is all about the streak."

Gathered around a makeshift table under a hastily erected tent in the parking lot of Torrey Pines Golf Course are some of the most famous faces and larynxes in televised golf. On my right is the éminence grise Ken Venturi, starting his thirty-third year in the tower, and two seats over the shamelessly mellifluous Jim Nantz, who did his first Masters at twenty-six and is just settling into his prime. On the other folding chairs are their supporting cast—Gary McCord, David Feherty, Peter Kostis, and Peter Oosterhuis, each a celebrity in his own right.

The only little-known face belongs to Kearns, the boy wonder producer of CBS golf and the one in charge of this whole traveling circus. Kearns is small and chubby, and the streak he is referring to belongs, of course, to

Tiger Woods, who arrived in La Jolla going for his seventh victory in a row, a streak that began at the end of '99 and carried over into 2000.

"At the moment, he's tied for twenty-second," says Venturi. "It doesn't look like it's going to continue." The afternoon broadcast of the third round of the Buick Invitational is only a couple of hours away and both he and Nantz are already in navy blazers, shirts and ties, and full makeup.

"Doesn't matter," replies Kearns, who is thirty-one and flashes a trace of the impatience the young have for the old. "Win or lose, it's about the epic quest, the pursuit of golfing history, and the significance of what he's already done. Jack couldn't win seven in a row. Neither could Arnie. Not even Hogan. So even if Tiger comes up short, we're going to ride him."

Kearns takes a gulp from a bucket-sized container of coffee, his third of the morning. As striking as Kearns's youth are his eyes, which are hyperalert and always at full aperture. "And if Phil does manage to hang on for once"—Mickelson currently leads by three—"it's about him breaking Tiger's streak, and about him not liking Tiger all that much, and having a Tiger complex, and feeling Tiger's hot breath on the back of his neck, et cetera, et cetera."

"You don't think people are a little tired of wall-to-wall

Tiger?" persists Venturi, and in the process perhaps exposing a little red neck beneath the tan.

"These telecasts are starting to feel like Tiger's home movies."

"According to the numbers, we're getting more viewers every week."

"Speaking of Urkel," says Nantz, "various sources inform me that Tiger has been spending a lot of time with women who might not be particularly appealing to Buick and Cadillac and our other sponsors."

"Can we be more specific?"

"Women in the adult entertainment industry," says Nantz with the same unhurried delivery and dulcet tones with which he describes the foliage at Amen Corner. "Strippers, a famous and not untalented porn star."

"Are your sources other strippers and porn stars?" asks McCord.

"Alas, no."

"For Christ's sake," says Feherty, "pro athletes have been hanging out with strippers since the beginning of time...give or take."

"David, are you suggesting that there were Paleolithic strippers?" asks Nantz without looking up from his notes.

"Yes. They were very pale."

"Let's hope the stories are exaggerated and stay rumors," says Kearns, "and if no one has any questions, or more gossip, please say hello to our newest on-course announcer, Travis McKinley."

Kearns's introduction takes me by surprise. In the last few days, I've come to realize that the flip side of having an agent with sufficient juice to get you a job simply by picking up the phone is that the person on the other end of the line isn't likely to be thrilled about getting the call. Kearns hasn't said a word to me since I arrived, and on the rare occasions when he's glanced in my direction, he's seemed to be searching my face for something he can't find.

"Lovely to meet you, Travis," says Nantz, still not looking up from his notes. "That win at Pebble over Jack and Raymond was one for the ages. And for future reference, that's usually my seat."

"Welcome to show business, kid," says Venturi with a warm smile. "Great to have you aboard."

"Don't get too attached to him," says Kearns, "it's only a tryout."

25

I'M STANDING BESIDE THE 12th tee watching Notah Begay tee off when there's a crackling in my headphones. "Nantz is coming to you in two," says Kearns. "He'll introduce you and then you're going to tell us about Begay's second shot. When the red light above the camera goes on, you're live."

Before the pre-pro meeting broke up, Kearns assigned me the threesome of Kevin Stadler, Steve Flesch, and Begay, and said he'd come to me sometime in the first hour. It was a canny choice. Stadler, a former Masters champion who often seems as disgusted with his game as any weekend hacker, is a great player and fan favorite, and Flesch is a talented southpaw, but I knew his real interest would be Begay. Begay was Tiger's teammate at Stanford, so talking about Begay is just one more way of talking about Tiger.

As soon as Begay's shot is in the air, me and cameraman

Mike Blundell chase after it like a pair of bird dogs. Twelve is a very long par 4 and Begay's drive bounces through the fairway into the left rough. After examining the lie (not great) and stepping off the distance (210 yards), I retreat fifty feet and wait. A quick sip of water alleviates my acute dry mouth but does little else. Second by second my anxiety grows until my mind is running amok inside my headset and turning against me. As much as the age-old dread of embarrassment and disgrace in front of a large audience, in this case approximately 2.4 million people, I fear my own perversity. What if for no other reason than the fact that it would be disastrously inappropriate, I succumb to a Tourette's-like outburst and start spouting obscenities?

A quick check of my watch shows it's been ninety seconds, but it's still a shock when Kearns is back in my left ear.

"Here we go—five seconds. Five…four…three… two…"

When he reaches one, the red light is flashing, and Nantz is in my other ear: "Now we're going to our newest on-course commentator and former U.S. Senior Open winner, Travis McKinley, who is on the twelfth hole."

Televised golf is the most tranquil of entertainments, a three-hour lullaby for an impromptu afternoon nap, but for those who are humming the lullaby, the process is sur-

prisingly raucous. With Kearns in my left ear and Nantz
in my right, I feel like I'm in the middle of a crowded bar.

"Travis, what does Notah have left for his second shot?"

"Well, Jim…" I say, and even in my fragmented state,
I note that my first two words of golf commentary were
"Well, Jim," which hardly seems auspicious.

"Despite a decent drive, Notah has two hundred ten
yards left from a very juicy lie."

"I guess you didn't see too many five-hundred-five-yard
par fours on the Senior Tour, did you, Travis?"

"Thank goodness. That would have fallen into the category of elder abuse. Twelve is a bear of a hole no matter
how young and strong you are. Anywhere near the green
would be a great result."

When Begay and his caddy reach the ball, where they
will spend the next twenty seconds considering the lie and
choosing a club, Kearns is back in my left ear. "Okay, now
we need some color."

Having spent the last two hours polishing a Begay
anecdote, I'm ready.

"Many people," I whisper, "are aware that Notah and
Tiger were teammates at Stanford, but their relationship
goes back to junior golf when Begay, the only Native
American player on the circuit, went out of his way to
befriend the only African-American. According to Tiger's
father, Begay, who is three years older, wanted Tiger to

know that he wasn't alone and would always have a friend, and that's quite something for a twelve-year-old to do."

"Well, let's see what Notah can do with this four-iron, Travis," says Nantz, and when the camera pulls away and focuses on Begay, I release an audible sigh. Despite some very shaky moments, I managed to lose my live television virginity without undo embarrassment. If I had a cigarette, I'd light it.

On Blundell's monitor, which shows the image viewers are seeing, Begay crouches beside the ball, takes one waggle, and steps away. When he returns the 4-iron to his caddy, Kearns is back in my left ear. "Travis, we need more color."

I thought I was done, that having cleared my first little hurdle, I could spend the next fifteen minutes or so luxuriating in relief, but now there are another twenty seconds to cover and I've used up my good anecdote. As Kearns counts me down, "...Five...four...," I frantically search my mind for material, "...three...," and come up empty. Desperation blooms into white-hot panic—"...two... one..."—and still nothing. For an interminable second, the airwaves are empty and I feel myself falling into a bottomless hole. In the distance, Notah's caddy lifts up his hand and pulls me out of the abyss with three fingers.

"Notah is switching to a three-iron," I say with more emotion than is usual to describe a club change. "Notah has been having issues with his back the last couple of weeks and the three will allow him to swing a little easier and take the pressure off his lower back. That's a great lesson for you amateurs—when you're facing a stressful shot, take one more club and swing easy."

It's the kind of serviceable little riff I've heard a thousand times over the years, but to me at that moment it sounds like poetry. Finally, Begay hits the goddamned shot and the focus of the telecast moves on.

26

FOR THE REST OF the day, Kearns has me handling exit interviews. This consists of corralling golfers as they walk off the 18th green and spoon-feeding them a couple of questions about their round before they duck into the scorers' tent. The challenge, which is not insignificant, is to get a professional golfer to say something. Anything. To discourage the player from waxing monosyllabic, you can't serve up a question that can be answered with a yes or no. In fact, you have to all but answer for them. Mostly it's a matter of making a quick observation and backing it up with a version of "How does it feel?" For example: "How does it feel to come back to Torrey Pines, where you played so well the last two years?" Or: "How crucial was that fourteen-footer you rolled in for par on thirteen in terms of maintaining the momentum of your round?" Or: "In the first couple of events you've struggled a bit on the weekend. How important was it to turn in a sixty-eight in the third round today?" Or, if you can handle one more: "You grew up and played college golf in the San Diego area. How good did it feel to play in front of so many old friends?" None of these softballs elicited anything the least bit surprising or interesting, but there were no awkward silences, so, all in all, it was a decent afternoon's work.

On Sunday, my apprenticeship resumed in the editing truck, where they had me lay down commentary over previously shot video. When you're watching a tournament and they cut to the sixth hole where Shigeki Maruyama, or some other golfer nowhere near the lead, is lining up a forty-five-footer, you can be pretty sure the ball is going to end up in the bottom of the hole. However, there was no way for the producers to have known that at the time, and unless the golfer was in the last couple of groups, no one was doing play-by-play.

To make the footage usable, a commentator does the voice-over later and presents it as if he witnessed it live. For a neophyte, it's a good exercise in proportionate moment milking. You want to get across the excitement and surprise of seeing that forty-five-foot bomb go in, but it's still just another inconsequential birdie on a Saturday by a golfer well outside the lead, so you can't go apeshit. You need to strike the right balance, and this little tone poem took multiple takes: "Maruyama just wants to cozy this forty-five-footer near the hole...the weight looks good...it's taking the break...could it be?...Yes! An unexpected birdie for Shigeki Maruyama."

In the evenings, I study tape of old telecasts in a way I never had before. Every twenty-three-foot putt by Phil Mickelson looks exactly the same as every other twenty-three-footer. Every three-hundred-yard drive bounds down the fairway like every other booming drive and every well-struck wedge dances around the flag in the same way. The only things that change are the context and the language.

Competent commentators never describe what the viewers can see for themselves, and the best and wittiest, like Feherty and McCord, view every bit of video and exchange as the chance for a bit of improv. The important thing for a rookie like me to keep in mind is that the bar is not that high. If you had something better to do or a little more energy, you probably wouldn't be sitting home on a Saturday afternoon and watching the third round of the Buick Invitational. But sometimes you don't, and believe me I know, because I've been there too. At times like that all the viewer is hoping for is to be transported from one moment to the next as painlessly as possible. For a few hours on weekend afternoons, our job is to be good company.

27

As a reward for not screwing up egregiously my first weekend and exceeding his low expectations, Kearns assigns me to follow Woods for three holes early on the back nine at Riviera. Even for someone who played the final eighteen of a senior major with Jack Nicklaus, witnessing Tiger up close is a thrill. There is a charisma to everything he does, even when he is doing nothing.

Blundell and I catch up to Tiger as he waits to hit his second shot on the par-4 ninth. For Woods, who is so often the longest off the tee and closest to the pin, waiting is something he does a great deal of, and every gesture from the way he nudges up the bill of his cap to the way he crosses his arms on his chest and chats to his famously belligerent caddy, Steve Williams, is elegant and streamlined. It's almost eerie to see a golfer so lacking in anxiety and self-doubt, so absent of tics and twitches, simultaneously in the moment and detached from it.

When it's finally his turn, Woods hits a piercing 185-yard 6-iron into the wind, and the quality of the strike, the tightness of the draw, and the confidence in the swing remind me of a quote from a college coach who saw Tiger play in high school. He said that if Tiger didn't do a thing in college or the pros and never teed it up again after the age of eighteen, he would still be the greatest golfer he had ever seen. I've watched him hit one shot in person and feel the same way.

Particularly amazing to me is the height he gets on his long irons and fairway woods. On the par-five 11th, a 320-yard drive leaves him 263 yards to the pin. Williams hands him an iron, and when I see the trajectory of his second shot, I think he's chosen to lay up, but it just keeps going…and going…and going until it lands on the green. His 3-iron has the trajectory of my 9-iron and lands so softly it's ridiculous.

On the next hole, Woods has a wedge to the green, and as I describe the upcoming shot, the wind abruptly changes directions and goes from hurting to helping. "The sudden change in conditions," I whisper, "might require a different club." The change also calls for a softer whisper, because my commentary, which would have been safely out of earshot seconds ago, is carried forward on the breeze, and by the way Woods and Williams turn sharply toward me, you might have thought I had just set off a firecracker.

Provoking the ire of Williams is not a good idea. It's like feeding the animals at the zoo. When Woods's wedge lands twelve feet from the hole, I'm hopeful that Williams will understand that there was no way of anticipating such a sudden change in wind direction and my rookie mistake will be forgiven, but Williams is not known for largesse. He is known for being large. Last year, after a gray-haired grandmother snapped a picture in Woods's backswing, Williams ripped the camera from her hands and hurled it into a pond.

Why should today be any different? I'm just grateful there's no water nearby. After replacing the divot, Williams leaves the bag in the fairway and stalks back toward me, and when he gets about halfway, I turn off my microphone so as to make my dressing-down a little less public. Williams doesn't stop until he is a tap-in from my face.

"Who are you?" asks Williams.

"Travis McKinley, nice to meet you."

"First day on the job?"

"Sixth, but let's not split hairs."

"If you ever screw up like that again or do anything to disturb Tiger, I will take that microphone and shove it up your ass."

"Thanks, Steve, I appreciate the heads-up."

As Williams stalks back to his bag, Nantz is in my right ear.

"What was that all about, Travis?"

"Steve was taking a moment to welcome me to the PGA Tour."

"Really? And how about that finger in your chest?"

"He was just flicking off a crumb from lunch."

28

I PEEL BACK THE aluminum wrapper and inhale the bracing bouquet. After a weekend of golf whispering, I need an antidote, a whiff of reality, a pungent reminder of who I am and where I come from, and what's more real than a Pink's Chicago Polish dog? Not much. At least not in West Hollywood.

I'm working my way through dog #1, savoring every molecule of sodium nitrate and phosphate, as well as my Dr. Brown's black cherry soda, when an eruption of squeals compels me to glance up from my tray. Crowding my table are three women not much younger than me, which seems mature considering the girlish pitch.

"No way," says their ringleader, "you're Travis McKinley. I saw you this afternoon with Tiger's caddy. That was hysterical. Do you mind if we take a picture of the four of us? We're huge golf fans."

"Okay," I say, and stand awkwardly among them while they enlist a fifth to capture the moment on film.

"What he's really like?" asks one of the others.

"Who?"

"Tiger, of course."

"I have no idea. I'm not even sure he knows. Or cares."

"Is he full of himself?"

"He kind of deserves to be, don't you think? He's twenty-five and the best golfer who ever lived."

"I guess so," she says.

Vaguely disappointed, the three wander out of the backyard. When they're safely out of sight, I return to my food, but a little bit of the Pink's magic is gone. In four years as a touring pro I was approached by strangers exactly three times, and in each case, I got an enormous kick out of it. Being recognized for something I was proud of made me feel great, but being cooed over for my work as a golf commentator is not nearly as gratifying. In fact, it feels like being busted. And no sooner do I return to my meal than I'm approached by another stranger, this time male. He wears a puzzled expression, and my first impression is that he's lost and needs directions.

"Do I know you?" he asks.

"Have you spent time in Winnetka, Illinois?"

"No."

"Probably not, then."

"You look very familiar."

"I've got a common face."

"No. I'm sure I recognize you."

"I used to be a professional golfer."

"Did you play on the regular tour?"

"The Senior Tour."

"I don't follow the Seniors. Too much of a yawn. I only watch the regular tour."

"Can't blame you for that. They're a lot better."

"*That*'s where I saw you. You're an announcer."

"Sometimes."

"One question."

"Okay?"

"What's Tiger really like?"

"He's a complete and utter asshole."

"I knew it! I just knew it! Thanks a lot. By the way, what's your name?"

"David Feherty. That's *F-e-h-e-r-t-y*."

29

THE NEXT MORNING, I get up at 6 a.m. and drive thirty miles to a scruffy public course in Encino. When someone finally arrives to open the pro shop up, I pay for two large buckets and carry them out to the far end of the range, where a couple of tufts of grass still cling to the dusty dirt. For the first time in nearly two months I hit golf balls.

To my surprise and relief, my tryout has not been a disaster. I understand the game and am capable of the occasional insight and witty retort, but there's a fundamental problem, which I have only become fully aware of in the last few days. I don't really like to talk, certainly not as a vocation, and when I do, half the things that slip out of my mouth make me cringe. What scares me is that pretty soon, I'll stop cringing, and without even noticing cross over from professional athlete to professional bullshitter.

That's why I'm so relieved to be hitting scuffed range rocks into the dusty featureless scrub, not thinking about anything except the sound of the ball hitting the club face.

For an hour, I have the entire crappy range to myself and couldn't be happier. Then a second pilgrim emerges from the pro shop. Along with his bucket, he carries a beat-up Sunday bag containing half a dozen mismatched forged irons and an even more obsolete Ben Hogan persimmon driver. Strapped to his bag with a pair of bungee cords is an ancient boom box, and Sinatra's "Nice 'n' Easy" is pouring out of it.

Although the entire space between me and the pro shop is empty, he walks all the way to my end of the range and sets up camp just past me on the last little piece of dirt to my left. He drops his bag, does a handful of yoga-looking stretches, then removes his clothes piece by piece until all he is wearing are golf shoes, socks, and a green Speedo. "I hate golfer's tan," he says, as if that's the only explanation required.

I handle his arrival in the same way I would if trapped beside a psychiatric outpatient on a bus or elevator. I avoid eye contact and pretend he isn't there, but the sound of his ball striking is too pure to resist a glance. His mind may not be sound, but his swing is perfect. I've spent the last six weeks observing up close the best golfers on the planet, and his swing is as good as any of them.

Maybe better. At every point in the arc, his club is exactly where it should be, and unlike with many golfers, even top pros, it arrives there naturally without last-second compensations or adjustments. And for someone in his late fifties, he hits it a ton.

I return my attention to my own swing, which feels flimsy and threadbare by comparison. After about ten minutes, I notice that my neighbor has taken a break. "I see you're having a little problem with your tempo," he says. "Frank isn't for everyone." He ejects the Sinatra cassette and pops in Bob Marley, and soon "No Woman No Cry" blasts out of the plastic speaker. "Try that."

I do. And he's right...on both counts. I *am* struggling with my tempo and the Wailers help. You may not be able to dance to reggae, but you can hit golf balls to it. The prominent bass lubricates your turn and makes it easier to sync the lower body and the arms. As we say on air, it's something you amateurs might want to try at home.

Twenty minutes later, he stops again. "Do you mind if I watch you hit a few?" Nearly half a century of experience and instinct suggests I should resist random input from a stranger, particularly one rocking a green Speedo, but he was right about the tempo and he was right about the reggae and I can see all too well that he doesn't have golfer's tan. "You got a nice little move," he says finally.

"You mean tight? Constricted? Constrained?"

"What the hell is wrong with you? I mean simple, efficient, repeatable. Don't ever change it. Have some faith in it. Invest in it. And FYI, you shouldn't be out here at the end of a range in Encino with a lunatic like me. You should be playing pro golf."

"So should you."

"Well, we're not talking about me now, are we?"

"I did…on the Senior Tour," I say. "I just lost my card."

"I'm talking about the real tour. Why spend your precious time playing with a bunch of old men? All that proves is who has happened to age a little better or who responds better to Advil."

"I had enough trouble with my contemporaries."

"Well, perhaps you need to raise your standards. In the meantime, word to Mother: go back to the beginning." And before I can ask him what he means and how I should get there, he starts to pack up.

"Travis McKinley," I say. "Thanks for everything."

"Seamus O'Casey. My pleasure. Keep it real."

Seamus's endorsement bolsters my confidence, and working on my game makes me feel like I haven't given up the ghost quite yet, that at least in some small way, I'm still a golfer and not just a golf whisperer. The next morning, I postpone my flight so I can work on it some more before returning to the arctic Midwest. Like yesterday, I arrive before the range opens and once again have it to myself until the familiar figure of O'Casey emerges from the clubhouse. Today, however, he carries himself differently, more formally, and it's reflected in his attire. He wears khaki trousers and a white polo shirt with a pink sweater draped over his shoulders, an ensemble that would pass muster at the snootiest country club, and there's no sight or sound of the boom box. Perhaps he's had a difficult evening, because he barely acknowledges me and when I say good morning, doesn't respond.

A few minutes later, when I brace myself and glance over my shoulder, I see that his stretching routine is new and apparently he is no longer hung up on golfer's tan because he hasn't removed a stitch. The swing, however, is just as pure and silky, although something is different and it's so fundamental it takes some time to realize what it is. He's hitting left-handed. Apparently, he doesn't just have one of the best swings in the world. He has two and they're mirror opposites. I stop hitting balls and gawk in amazement.

"Hey, pal, don't you have anything better to do?"

"Seamus, I can't believe how well you hit it left-handed."

"Do I know you?"

"Seamus, it's Travis. We met yesterday."

"My name isn't Seamus. It's Sean. I've never seen you before in my life."

30

IN EARLY MARCH, THE PGA caravan rolls into Coral Springs for the start of the Florida swing. It's my first event without Tiger in the field, and the buzz of anticipation that filled the air in La Jolla and Los Angeles is gone. The same tractor-trailers, production trucks, and high-tech vans fill the parking lot, but the gaffers, electricians, and production assistants coming in and out of them move with less urgency, and at our pre-pro meeting, the torpor recalls a midafternoon high school study hall. I half expect Nantz and Venturi to start firing spitballs at each other.

"If a tree falls on a golf course, and Tiger isn't there to hear it, did it happen?" asks Feherty, staring soulfully into the distance, and McCord jerks his chin off his chest like a man startled awake by his own snoring. "Did David just say something profound? Or was I dreaming?"

"It's not funny," says Kearns, "and unless we can drum

up some interest, the only noise we'll hear is the sound of people reaching for their remotes and turning the channel. If anyone has any ideas—any *serious ideas*—about how we can hang on to our viewers, please share them."

Kearns's call for seriousness makes the atmosphere around the table seem even more like high school, and for the next couple of minutes the most famous announcers and commentators in golf stare sheepishly at their hands. Everyone except me, because unlike my neighbors, I'm sitting on an idea. I just don't want to voice it. In fact, I have resisted disclosing it for several days.

"Hugo Caldecker," I say. As soon as the name is out of my mouth, I regret it, but when neither Kearns nor anyone else at the table responds, I keep right on talking. "Caldecker," I explain, "is a thirty-two-year-old former All-American playing this week on a sponsor's exemption. What makes his story unusual is that four years ago, his right leg was amputated from the knee down, and very few people are aware of it."

The only reason I happen to know is that Caldecker and I both played our college golf for Northwestern and I heard about the accident from my former college coach, Ted Winsky. Winsky told me that Caldecker is determined not to publicize his handicap, so I know he is the last person who would want his courage and determination lauded on network TV. He has declined interviews even from his small-town local weekly.

Unfortunately, Caldecker is the only ammunition I've got, and as someone two-thirds of the way through a six-week tryout whose outcome is far from certain, I don't have the character not to use it. If this tryout doesn't pan out, what are my options? Become a teaching pro at a country club? Not with my social skills. Open my own driving range and go into competition with Big Oaks? I don't even know how to balance a checkbook. Partner up with Louie and start Louie and Travis Dog Walkers? Of the three ideas, that may be the least farfetched, no pun intended, and anything is preferable to going back to *The Journey of a Journeyman*.

Upon hearing the first details of Caldecker's story, Kearns snaps to attention. His eyes, which are always held wide open, widen further and his cheeks redden, and watching Kearns become a fuller, more vivid version of himself confirms my misgivings.

"This is wonderful," says Kearns so softly he seems to be talking to himself. "A gift from the universe. McKinley, you're going to cover every swing *and step* Caldecker takes, and we're going to milk this story for every last drop of emotion and pathos." To underline his point, he holds his small fists together and twists them in opposite directions, as if wringing the water from a sopping towel. "Let's just hope to Christ he makes the cut."

31

On Thursday morning, Caldecker, Ted Tryba, and Tommy Tolles have a 7:18 tee time. Other than Caldecker's wife and young son, the only people waiting to see them off are me and my cameraman Mike Blundell. Although TV coverage won't start until Saturday, we will be following him for thirty-six holes, gathering material that could be useful for the weekend. Tryba and Tolles react to our presence with mild curiosity and surprise, Caldecker with a wry smile.

Caldecker has retaught himself to walk so well that the difference in his gait is barely perceptible. As he steps to the blue markers and plants his tee in the manicured turf, his strides are brisk and fluid and so are his practice swings. What distinguishes him is his face, a creased map of all he's been through, the strength he has derived from it as well as the cost. It's the kind of face you rarely come across on the PGA tour, and although all three players are about the same age, Tryba and Tolles seem childlike by comparison.

Caldecker is also the most nervous of the three because he has the most at stake this morning. As someone with no status on tour who got into the field on a sponsor's exemption, the pressure to take advantage of his rare opportunity is enormous. Under the circumstances, Caldecker and his game hold up well.

Determined to avoid the big number, he plays more conservatively than his playing partners and churns out one carefully plotted par after another, and his one-under-par 71 puts him smack in the middle of the field. So far at least, his leg does not appear to be a factor.

Friday brings more of the same. Caldecker continues to play within himself, finding the fairways off the tee and the center of the greens on his approaches. Fortunately, he makes a couple more putts, and after 14, he is three under for the day, four under for the tournament. For the second day in a row, the leg appears to be less of an issue than the usual rookie tensions, but as they leave 15, his caddy has to wait for him to catch up and both Blundell and I can see the strain in his eyes. Over the next three holes, Caldecker and his caddy walk slower and slower, and on 18, with the clubhouse in sight, Caldecker limps noticeably for the first time in the tournament. Nevertheless, his 68, and two-day today total of 139, put him comfortably inside the cutline and ensure he will be around for the weekend, and the only one as relieved as Caldecker is Kearns.

When he walks off 18, Blundell and I intercept him for a brief interview to be aired the next day. "Congratulations, Hugo, on two solid rounds of golf. How does it feel," I ask, "after all you've been through, to finally make your first PGA cut?"

The phrase "all you've been through" elicits the same wry smile I saw on the first tee. If he had any doubts as to why CBS would assign a crew to cover the first thirty-six holes of an unknown rookie playing on a sponsor's exemption, they have just been erased.

"Relieved," he says. "I don't know when I'll get another chance to do this again."

"Until the last couple of holes, you were moving well, but you seemed in some discomfort on the last few holes. How much was the leg bothering you today?"

"I'm not going to talk about the leg," says Caldecker, and brings the interview to an abrupt close. He pivots and limps off, but before he steps into the scorers' tent, he turns back and offers one last withering glance.

32

WHEN CBS GOES ON air at 3 p.m. on Saturday, Caldecker's group has reached the 7th tee. Making the cut has freed him up to finally fire at some pins, and three quick birdies have vaulted him from thirty-second place, where he began his day, to fifteenth. After Caldecker hits a solid drive, I introduce him to viewers.

"Since Thursday morning, I've been following a special young golfer named Hugo Caldecker. Caldecker played his college golf at Northwestern, where he was a two-time All-American. After graduation, he turned pro and spent the next three years playing the mini-tours in Asia, Australia, and South America. On a rainy night outside Bogotá, Colombia, in February 1995, the car in which he was a passenger slid off the road into a tree. In the next few days, the cut on Caldecker's right calf became so badly infected, Colombian doctors had to amputate from the knee down. Over the next two years there would be more surgeries and months and months of rehab. He had to learn to walk on his prosthesis and then learn a whole new swing. On Thursday, his leg held up well, but by the end of yesterday's round he was limping noticeably, and we'll be looking closely to see how much his leg is bothering him today."

On 8, Caldecker rolls in a downhill sixteen-footer for another birdie and Kearns comes right back to me. "When he arrived on Monday, Caldecker's goals were modest," I say, "to make his first PGA cut and earn a paycheck for his young family, his wife, Ronnelle, and their towheaded toddler, Casper, but with his fourth birdie of the day, Caldecker and his family get to see his name on a PGA leaderboard. After all he has been through, it has to be a thrilling moment for this courageous young man." As I whisper into America's ear, I keep seeing Kearns's fist wringing his imaginary towel, and although I like to think I stay well short of that, I know it's not by much.

Caldecker pars 9 and 10. After another solid drive on 11, his leg buckles on the follow-through. When he steps off the tee, his face is pale and his jaw clenched, and fifty yards later he's limping badly again.

Kearns, who is monitoring the action from a production truck, responds to Caldecker's distress like a shark smelling blood and within seconds is back in my headset:

"The game is on," he says. "Every time I come back to you I need an update on the leg. Is it getting worse? How much worse? From here on, it's about pain and courage. And don't let up."

"Caldecker has a hundred and twenty-five yards to the green. On the walk from the tee, it was obvious that Caldecker is hurting.... Caldecker's caddy slips two more Advils into his palm. Then hands him his wedge.... Caldecker grimaces on the follow-through but the strike is clean... it's all over the flag... less than ten feet for birdie... he crouches gingerly behind the ball... pulls himself upright. One practice stroke... Yes! Hugo Caldecker is tied for the lead of the Honda Classic!"

On the last three holes, I keep reaching for the towel like a jockey going to the whip on the home stretch. "On every hole, Caldecker seems to be in more pain... at this point the only things getting him to the house are guts and painkillers... let me change that to guts alone, because there's no evidence the painkillers are doing much good... those pars on sixteen, seventeen, and eighteen were anything but routine and his four-under sixty-eight is one of the most courageous rounds I've ever witnessed."

Once again, Blundell and I position ourselves to intercept Caldecker coming off 18. Before we can subject him to another interview, a cart races up to the back of the green and whisks Caldecker away. "That Caldecker required a cart to travel the short distance between the eighteenth green and the scorers' tent," I say, "indicates just what kind of pain he is in."

I'm relieved that Caldecker has eluded us. Kearns is furious and makes up for the lack of an interview by having Nantz take viewers through a hole-by-hole recap of Caldecker's round. He intercuts video of Caldecker's well-struck shots and holed putts with close-ups of his painful steps.

33

CALDECKER ISN'T THE ONLY one whose stock has risen overnight. When coverage resumes Sunday afternoon, Nantz introduces viewers "to Travis McKinley, the newest member of the CBS family." Then Kearns puts me on camera, as I stand microphone in hand between the blue markers of the first tee. As he counts me down, "Five...four...three...two...one," I remind myself that I don't have to whisper.

"From the tips, TPC Heron plays seven thousand, three hundred yards. That's four and a half miles as the crow flies. Golfers, however, don't fly, and on the ground, it's more like six miles. Each mile is two thousand steps. If Hugo Caldecker is going to have a chance to win his first golf tournament, he will have to take twelve thousand of them, and for Caldecker, who lost part of his right leg as a result of complications from a car accident in South

America four years ago, each step is not only more difficult than that of his competitors, it's harder than the one before it."

On Friday and Saturday, Caldecker's steps became labored and painful toward the end of each round. On Sunday he is limping badly off the second tee. At every opportunity, Caldecker takes the weight off his left leg. On the second tee, he avails himself of a nearby bench. On the third, with no bench in sight, he sits on his golf bag, and after tapping in for par on the 4th, he sits on the bank behind a green. As he hobbles up fairways, he uses his 2-iron as a cane, and in between shots, he lifts his left leg and balances himself against his bag or leans directly on his caddy, Samuel Montgomery.

He also takes strength from his huge gallery. The attention given to Caldecker and his handicap, the bulk of it piped into American homes through my microphone, has won him a legion of new fans who roar his every shot and chant his name. At times it's difficult to watch, yet somehow Caldecker gets through the first five holes without surrendering a bogey or his share of the lead.

"You can just imagine what a win would mean to this young man," I whisper as Caldecker limps off the fifth tee. "The big paycheck, the two-year exemption, the invitation to the Masters and the trip to Hawaii for the Tournament of Champions, as well as tangible proof that all his hard work has not been in vain. For now, though, he has to find a way to put aside all thoughts of what a win would mean and focus on playing one shot at a time and putting one foot in front of the other."

In my headset, Kearns barks his approval: "One foot in front of the other—love it—and don't let up." After Caldecker pars three more holes, Kearns unveils a graphic that he runs at the bottom of the screen whenever Caldecker is on camera and tabulates live every additional step, and Nantz updates viewers when he reaches 2,000, 3,000, 4,000. Caldecker grinds out another par to finish the front nine in even par 36. "In sports, we like to think the playing field is level, but for the first nine holes, Caldecker has been playing uphill. Nevertheless, he is halfway home."

By the start of the back nine, Caldecker can barely put any weight on the left leg even when he is swinging. Unable to make a full follow-through, he loses a third of his distance and his driver barely carries two hundred yards. Where the co-leader Dudley Hart is hitting wedges and short irons to the green, Caldecker is hitting fairway woods. Yet by missing his approach shots in the right places, he keeps finding ways to salvage par, and when Hart three-putts the 16th hole, Caldecker has the lead to himself.

"This is not just one of the bravest rounds I've ever

seen, it's one of the smartest and most disciplined. He and Montgomery have obviously done a great deal of thinking about this round in advance, and again and again Caldecker has left himself uphill chips and putts. With only two holes to go, Caldecker leads the Honda Classic. He's almost home. Can he hang on?"

On the short par-four 17th, Caldecker bunts his driver 180 yards into the middle of the fairway and limps after it. "He's got one hundred eighty-eight yards to the green," I say, and Montgomery has given him a 3-wood. Once again, he's just trying to get this somewhere in front of the green. Two holes ago, Caldecker stopped taking practice swings, but this time he takes one and then another and then puts the club back in the bag and reaches out for Montgomery, who gently lowers him to the ground. He is sitting on the grass when a PGA tour official pulls up beside him in a golf cart. The official says something into his walkie-talkie and seconds later two more carts arrive. After a short discussion, Caldecker climbs onto one cart, the caddy onto another, and the two carts speed off toward the clubhouse.

"It's heartbreaking," I say. "With little less than five hundred yards to the clubhouse and what could have been his first win on the PGA Tour, Hugo Caldecker could not take another step."

34

"WHAT ARE YOU DOING?" Kearns barks through my head-set. "You're letting him get away! We're not done yet. We need an interview with him right now."

"You want me to ask him how he feels?"

"That's exactly what I want you to ask him."

Everyone who has been watching already knows how he feels, I think. *He's devastated. And in excruciating pain.* "Can't we leave the guy alone for a few minutes?"

"No. It's unpleasant but you have to do it. That's why it's called a job."

I wave over a tour official and Blundell and I comman-deer his cart. The only reason Caldecker is still in sight is because his cart stopped to pick up his wife and son, and from behind I can see them collapsed into each other. Unfortunately, there is no longer any need for Caldecker to sign his card. By not completing the round, Caldecker, who was leading after seventy holes, will automatically finish last in the field, and earn the same amount as if he had withdrawn Friday night.

We follow his cart past the scorers' tent and then to the clubhouse, where he pulls onto a large, nearly empty patio. When we catch up to them, the family is sitting at a small table at the far end. He and his wife are sobbing as their four-year-old son looks on, distressed and bewildered.

Kearns is back in my headset: "Travis, where are you? . . . You find him?"

For a second, I don't answer, and I wish I hadn't. "Yes."

"Excellent. We're going to a commercial and then back to you."

Two minutes later, he counts me off.

"Hugo, very sorry to bother you right now. I hope you realize how much what you did these past four days has meant to people, how much your courage and determination will continue to mean to them." When Caldecker doesn't answer, I continue: "When did you realize you weren't going to be able to finish the round?"

"The first step I took when I got out of bed."

"When you waved over the official on seventeen, you were so close to the finish line. What did you tell him?"

"I told him I was going to pass out. I really didn't want to do that in front of my wife and son. Not to mention my friends and parents watching on TV. The hell with that."

"Hugo, I know it may not seem like it now, but you accomplished a great deal this weekend. You came within two holes of winning on the PGA tour. I'm sure other sponsors will be offering you exemptions. Will you try again?"

"What's the point?"

"Maybe you can make some adjustments that will make walking less painful."

Caldecker flashes a look of disgust. "You don't think we've been trying that for the last year?"

The left leg of Caldecker's slacks flaps at the bottom, and scanning the table, I see his prosthetic with his golf shoe still attached to it sitting on the wrought-iron chair. Both the prosthetic and the white shoe are covered in blood, and they are dripping into a red puddle beneath the chair.

"You got your little interview," says Caldecker, "could you please give us some time alone?"

The seven-second delay enables Kearns to cut away before Caldecker's request for privacy. That evening ESPN ends their telecast with Blundell's video of blood dripping off the shoe onto the patio. Blundell captured audio, too, and you can hear the drops hit the cement. I'm in my hotel room sipping a beer when Kearns calls.

"Travis, you did some incredible work this weekend. Our ratings for the tournament were only two points less than the average when Tiger is in the field. I had my doubts but you proved me wrong. You've got a real future in this business."

"I don't think so."

"Trust me on this one, Travis. You're a natural."

"I hope you're wrong about that, Burt. In any case it doesn't matter. Because I quit."

35

HOME, HOME ON THE range, where the ex-pro and the assistant pro play.

On a perfect morning in late June, the kind that makes Chicagoans forget the endless winter, Louie and I are set up in our usual spot in the far rear corner of the Creekview Country Club driving range. We've spent much of the last two and a half months here, me pounding balls and practicing my short game, and Louie chasing crows and hedgehogs and sleeping in the sun. I can't speak for Louie, but I feel like I still have a little game left, although to be honest it's starting to feel a bit hypothetical, since I don't know when, if ever, I'll get a chance to play it again.

One reason I'm feeling hopeful despite my unemployment status is the encouragement I received from my driving range neighbor in Encino. Yeah, he was rocking a green Speedo, but he also sported one of the best swings I've ever seen on either tour, and I'd rather get an endorsement from a maniac who knows what he's talking about than from someone of unquestioned mental stability who doesn't, although I concede that ideally, you're looking for both.

"Go back to the beginning," he advised, and since returning to Winnetka I've often pondered what he meant. On the chance that he was referring to technique, I've refocused on the fundamentals handed down to me over forty years ago by my late grandfather. Every morning before I hit a single ball, I re-create Pop's earliest lessons about setup, alignment, posture, and grip. But perhaps he had something else in mind. Maybe he was trying to steer me toward a psychological or emotional beginning. A fresh start, a blank page? In any case, my searching has done me no harm, and although I can't point to a dramatic breakthrough, my game feels as sharp as ever, and I'm hitting the ball as long and well as any fifty-four-year-old has a right to.

Unfortunately, the only chances I've had to brandish my game are in my twice-weekly money matches with assistant pro Cameron Booth and his long-hitting college golf pal Jonah Cooper. Do I feel bad fleecing twentysomethings barely earning minimum wage for $200 and $300 a pop? Not really, particularly since I'm giving them thirty years and a stroke a side. Still, the sharp edge of my game feels underutilized, like I'm all dressed up with nowhere to go.

36

ON THE OTHER HAND, after four years on the road, having nowhere to go is kind of the point. Before I head to the range, I drop off Noah at his day camp and, before I pick him up, gather the ingredients for dinner. Three or four nights a week, I do the cooking as well, and tonight after serving my signature SFM, simple fish meal—roast salmon, sautéed vegetables, potatoes *dauphinoise*—we decide to extend our evening by going into town for ice cream at our beloved Dairy Queen.

On these mild summer evenings, I'm often struck by the civic harmony and goodwill in ice cream lines. People exercising their right to vote for the ice cream or frozen milk of their choice may be the most hopeful example of democracy we have left. There is no other place where the various segments of our population smile at each other as openly, or tolerate each other's unruly kids as patiently. At

DQ, it's pretty obvious that at the end of the day we all want the same thing, which is to get our chocolate-dipped cones from the order window and into our mouths before they melt all over us.

Our calories consumed, we burn off a fraction immediately by walking the half dozen blocks to the shopping district and extend our municipal experience inside the cavernous Blockbuster. Crossing the threshold of a Blockbuster on a whim, without a list negotiated and agreed upon in advance, is a dangerous game. There are too many choices and so many of them suck and when it comes to entertainment, common ground between a man, a woman, and a nine-year-old boy is elusive. After fifteen minutes, I'm just going through the motions, placing one foot in front of the other and tossing out a title, which I know will be rejected by one or both, and not always nicely.

I'm getting a steady diet of "no way," "you got to be kidding," and "you couldn't pay me enough to sit through that," and my gloom as I squint at the alphabetically arranged DVDs reminds me of weaving through thick woods looking for an errant tee shot. If you stumble on the ball, it's a minor miracle, and that's the way I feel when I cross the border between "action" and "comedy" and spot at the bottom of a skinny black spine the tiny snapshots of Derek Smalls, David St. Hubbins, and Nigel

Tufnel, each looking more smug and clueless than the other, and above them the cheesy 3-D typeface with the gratuitous umlaut over a consonant.

"Sarah, I think Noah is ready."

"For what?"

"Spinal Tap."

37

Minutes after inserting the DVD, I realize I'm wrong. *This Is Spinal Tap* is a fictional documentary about the ill-fated American tour of a particularly moronic heavy metal band. *Spinal Tap* is wildly inappropriate for a nine-year-old. Sarah and I are lucky a representative from Children's Services doesn't barge in in the middle of their anthem "Big Bottom," sample lyric *"My baby fits me like a flesh tuxedo / I'm going to sink her with my pink torpedo."* But in spite of the occasional eye roll and "Really, Travis?" from Sarah, everyone, including her, is laughing so uproariously, I don't have the heart or the mandate to pull the plug.

At this point it's too late anyway. A better strategy, I decide, is to act like it's no big deal, and of course it isn't. And as I rationalize to myself, if you're going to expose your third grader to one hour and twenty-two minutes of

Advanced Placement sex ed, it might as well arrive in the form of a comic masterpiece.

What I wasn't quite prepared for was how quickly he would absorb every skit, lyric, and scrap of dialogue and how completely it would colonize every cranny of his brain. "You can't really dust for vomit" becomes an all-purpose motto, repeated ad nauseam and apropos of nothing, and he asks for his bread to be toasted to 11, and when I drop him at camp, "Love you, have a good day" is replaced by "But enough yakking, let's boogie."

On the plus side, the band's disastrous live performance of "Stonehenge," at which an eighteen-inch rather than eighteen-foot model of the monument is lowered to the stage, inspires him to take out a library book on the prehistoric landmark, and the next weekend at breakfast, he corrects a piece of misinformation from the movie. "Druids had nothing to do with the construction of Stonehenge," he informs us. "Druids didn't arrive until a thousand years after they were built." See, it all turned out fine in the end, and I'm a wonderful parent, and as I flip pancakes and Noah reads about "trilithons" and Sarah pores over her *Tribune,* a wave of domestic well-being washes over me.

"How about," I say, "we take advantage of the fact that I'm home this summer and everyone is in such fine shape by going to the actual Stonehenge. And while we're at it, we can go to Scotland. We haven't taken a family vacation in years. Let's get out of town. See a bit of the world. Expand our horizons."

Noah embraces the idea immediately, as he would any proposal inspired by *This Is Spinal Tap*. Sarah studies me with the same quizzical smile I've noticed now and then when I bring dinner to the table. I wouldn't presume to interpret a woman's smile, but if I had to attempt a translation it would be something along the lines of, "Who is this impostor residing in the body of Travis McKinley, and is there any chance he'll stick around for a while?"

38

THREE WEEKS LATER, THE four of us are standing in the parking lot of EuroTour Rentals, just outside Gatwick International Airport, picking up the keys to our large white van. England is hardly exotic travel. Nevertheless, everything looks different and smells different—maybe it's the gas they use—and there is a bracing snap of foreignness in the early-morning air.

Since I blurted out my proposal, our travel plans have been revised and refined. The first issue was Louie and our unwillingness to abandon the pooch for several weeks while the rest of us go gallivanting around the United Kingdom. For a while we leaned toward a full-service motor home, complete with comfortable beds, a kitchen, and a bathroom with shower. The deal breaker was the ten-minute video detailing how to empty and wash the plastic receptacle connected to the toilet. At that point, we decided we'd take our chances on dog-friendly bed-and-breakfasts and small hotels and a camper van, which in a pinch can sleep four.

Thank goodness, we lowered our sights. Keeping this large unfamiliar vehicle on the correct side of the road is challenge enough. Conceptually, driving on the left instead of the right doesn't sound hard, but the old pattern is so ingrained and the consequences for screwing up so severe that in the first couple of hours, the phrase *RIGHT equals DEATH* is never far from my mind, and after navigating several tricky intersections, I have a cramp in my left hand from clutching the wheel so tightly. If Sarah weren't reading the signs and navigating, I don't think I could handle it.

Stonehenge is near Amesbury, 90 miles southwest of London. Including a quick stop for breakfast, it takes us three hours, and when we turn off the highway into a huge parking lot lined with tour buses, it's just after noon. Before we disembark, we reinsert the soundtrack of *This Is Spinal Tap* and play "Stonehenge." The song begins with an intro spoken by Nigel, and whatever drama it delivers is derived from the smoke machine:

In ancient times, hundreds of years before the dawn of history, lived a strange race of people, the Druids. No one knows who they were or what they were doing, but their legacy remains hewn into the living rock of Stone-henge....

Then we pull off our sweaters, revealing the Spinal Tap T-shirts underneath. Sarah wears basic black with the name of the band across the chest. Noah's has an illustration of Nigel's amplifier set to 11, and I've got the "Tap into America" concert tee, listing the scheduled tour dates, five of which are labeled CANCELLED. I don't let Sarah put a T-shirt on Louie because clothes on a dog are undignified.

After a last check in the mirror, we step out of the van. We line up at the Welcome Center and purchase tickets. Then we line up again for the bus that ferries you to the site. Then we file off and walk out toward the circle of stones in the center of a large open plain. "We did it," says Noah. "We're actually here."

One minute you're in the kitchen flipping pancakes and talking shit. The next you're in a field in southern England gazing up at stones the approximate color, size, and shape of whales. Even more than the immensity of the stones themselves, we're gawking at the scale of the undertaking and the grunt labor and engineering required to transport them hundreds of miles, prop them up, and plant them in this near-perfect circle. This may be the first public works project on record, and it occurs to me that while we would all love to leave a lasting impression, what we really need is something to do while we're here.

The realization is a little scary. As much as I've been enjoying dropping off and picking up Noah at camp, doing the grocery shopping, and roasting the occasional piece of fish or chicken, I suspect it's not going to be enough of a project for long. Sooner or later, I'm going to have to get out there and wrestle with the big rocks again.

As we're all trying to haul aboard this epic scene, each in our own way, I notice another couple with a boy and a girl a bit older than Noah. The father, who has long hair parted in the middle and circular wire-rimmed glasses, has the air of a doddering old rock star. As he gets closer, I see why. It's Ozzy Osbourne. When he's safely out of earshot, I share the celebrity sighting with Sarah and Noah.

"See that guy over there? He's Ozzy Osbourne, and way back in the mists of time, when Druids roamed the land, he was the front man of a heavy metal band called Black Sabbath, and they were Spinal Tap before Spinal Tap."

"Like Stonehenge was the pyramids before the pyramids."

"Pretty much. Not only that, Ozzy bit the head off a bat."

"No way," says Noah.

"Yes way."

"Travis, was this really necessary?" asks Sarah.

"Absolutely. It's an important part of rock history."

39

EARLY THE NEXT MORNING, the courtesy van begins its trip north. We stop for tea and crumpets in a thatched-roof village in Oxfordshire and for lunch at a café on a canal in Manchester, where, at the end of the nineteenth century, England first turned away from that rural life of the Cotswolds and cast its lot for better or worse with the Industrial Revolution. Sarah, our on-board librarian, informs us that Manchester was once the largest cotton-producing center in the world and the scene of the first bread and labor riots. Noah is more taken by the fact that its residents are called Mancunians, or Mancs, and their word for chewing gum is *chuddy.*

Near Carlisle, the road climbs into the Cheviot Hills, and just beyond Longtown in northern Cumbria, we pass a road sign reading FÀILTE GU ALBA, Scottish Gaelic for WELCOME TO SCOTLAND. At the first opportunity, I pull off at the tiny town of Canobie so that I can take my first steps on ancestral sod. It might not be up there with Armstrong on the moon, but I feel an unanticipated shiver of excitement and maybe also of recognition.

Across from the desk in my office is an engraving of a farmhouse that has been passed down across several generations. The house, made of rough-hewn wooden planks, is built into the side of a hill and shaded by two V-shaped apple trees, and according to family legend was the birthplace of my great-great-grandfather Jamie McKinley. On the back of the engraving is the barely legible notation *Balquhidder, summer, 1887*. Balquhidder is in the council area of Stirling, in the county of Perthshire, between the two slightly larger towns of Strathyre and Lochearnhead. About an hour and fifteen minutes north of Glasgow, we pull off the A8 and travel the one-lane rural roads in search of the farmhouse rendered in the picture.

As we've traveled north, the landscape has grown more rugged and less peopled, and in the next hour we see fewer than half a dozen houses, none of which is a match. We do, however, pass a hill with a similar slope and landscape to the ones in the engraving, and when we circle back and park, Sarah spots the apple trees and the charred base of a chimney. Eventually, by matching the scene with the picture of the engraving on Sarah's phone, we confirm with a fair degree of certainty that it is the remains of my great-great-grandfather's house.

For the next several hours, we walk the property in every direction and get the lay of the land, which has stark, desolate beauty. Then we buy some provisions in the nearest town and picnic on what once was probably the kitchen of the old house. Halfway through a bottle of wine, Sarah and I decide to park the van on the old homestead and spend the night.

"Noah," I say, "now we know where we're from…at least to some degree."

40

WE SLEEP IN—THERE'S no early checkout time in the courtesy van—and don't get back on the road till early afternoon. The farther north we go the more dramatic the landscapes, but as taken as I am by the iconic terrain, the scenic bits of Scotland aren't flying by fast enough. In a matter of hours, I'll be teeing it up for the first time in the land where not just my earliest forebears, but golf itself, were conceived, and as much as I'm enjoying the braes (hills) and the burns (streams) and the lochs (lakes), it's hard to think of much else.

Back in Winnetka, when the itinerary was still in its early stages, everyone conceded I couldn't visit Scotland without playing at least one round. My first thought, of course, was St. Andrews, where nearly a thousand years ago the first shepherd hit a stone with a crooked staff, but the Old Course will be hosting the Open Championship at the end of the month and is closed to the public until after the tournament. My second choice was Royal Dornoch in the Scottish Highlands, where we're heading now. While less renowned, Royal Dornoch is nearly as revered by cognoscenti, and its remoteness keeps away all but the most committed pilgrims.

As the afternoon ticks by, we push due north past Perth and Dundee and Inverness, and even with a heavy right foot, we don't arrive in Dornoch till nearly five. At most golf destinations, such a late arrival would require postponing, but in this case it doesn't even cause any uptight urgency, because in mid-July in Dornoch, which sits on the same latitude as Juneau, Alaska, the sun doesn't set till after 10 p.m., which gives us plenty of time to check into our B&B and have a quick look at the town.

A couple of blocks past the cathedral is the aptly named Golf Road, which dead-ends after a few hundred yards at a small parking lot. To the left is an unassuming white stone clubhouse. To the right are the first tee and the putting green, and between them a large, high sign announces that you have finally reached the Royal Dornoch Golf Club. Except for the lone figure on the putting green, there is not another golfer in sight.

Even without the sign, there is no mistaking the fact that you have reached the promised land. The course sits at the northernmost point of the known golfing world high above Dornoch Firth and the North Sea, and you feel the freedom of all that ocean and sky, combined with a rare tranquility. Imagine a course as beautiful as Augusta National without the color correction, and as epic as Pebble, where without a tee time you can drive up at 5:30 p.m. on Friday afternoon, park your van in the empty lot, and walk on.

41

WITHIN MINUTES, ME AND the single on the putting green, a man named Andy—in his early sixties with a pencil-thin moustache—head to the first tee, and after a long day on the road, Sarah, Noah, and Louie are happy to tag along and stretch their legs. It's classic Scottish weather, cool and blustery, rain one instant, sunshine the next, and yet somehow the conditions seem perfect, and it's clear that my fellow travelers are enjoying the spongy turf and ocean air as much as me.

The first half dozen holes are on the upper portion of the course. Although you feel and see the ocean from nearly every hole, there's also the sense of being protected and shielded from it, and with no one ahead of or behind us, there's scant evidence of humanity. I know the course has been played for three hundred years, but as we stand on the 7th tee, a nearly 500-yard par 4 tucked away on a high plateau bordered on both sides by thick gorse, I feel less like a golfer than like an explorer who has stumbled onto some mythical uncharted territory. I feel like Columbus wading ashore in the New World.

In such a magical setting, I'd be content just scraping it along and keeping up with Andy, who plays off a 3, but in fact, I'm doing quite a bit better than that. Scottish golf, which plays closer to the ground, fits my swing and my eye, and my game shows the benefit of those three months on the range. The swing feels good and although I didn't roll a single ball on the practice green, so does the putter, as if the pace of these greens is part of my genetic inheritance. How else to explain the fact that I've only needed eight putts on the first six holes?

"I'm afraid to ask what you're shooting," says Sarah when I touch her hand on the 7th tee. "I haven't seen you miss a shot or a putt."

"Give me a kiss and I'll try not to think about it."

With our second shots on 8, we finally drop out of the clouds. For the next nine holes the course hugs the beach and plays to a track of cawing gulls and breaking surf, and the wind picks up. Like the teammate of a pitcher working on a no-hitter, Andy fastidiously avoids any mention of my string of birdies. He fills me in on his plumbing business in Edinburgh, his two married daughters, his wife, who at this very moment is probably buying an overpriced antique in town. And when I hole a long chip on 7 for yet another birdie, he asks, "What do you think of John Daly's chances at St. Andrews?"

"With JD, anything is possible," I say. "Good or bad."

"That's the wonder of him, isn't it? He doesn't give a toss."

On 16, the fairway climbs back up into the sky, and when you reach the green and turn back, it feels like the entire northern coast of Scotland is stretched out at your feet. Before I hit, I find Sarah's eyes again. I finish par, birdie, birdie, and when our last putts are safely holed, Andy reaches for my hand and slaps me on the shoulder. "Andy," I say, "this is a round I'll never forget."

"I would hope the hell not."

After Andy apologizes for not being able to buy me a drink—he has a long drive home ahead of him—he hands the card to Sarah and says, "I'm going to entrust this to you." And while I get reacquainted with Noah and the pooch, Sarah does the math.

"You shot a sixty-one," she says, and shows me the card, which is signed and annotated. In tight precise script, he has written *Andy* under *Player A* and *The Yank* under *Player B,* and each of my nine birdies is circled.

"I had no idea."

"Bullshit."

"Okay. I had a pretty good idea."

Inside the pro shop, Sarah gets a recommendation for dinner from the assistant pro. "While I've got you, what's the course record?"

"That would be sixty-two," he says.

"Then you might want to make a copy of this," she says, and hands him the scorecard. "Sixty-one, straight out of the parking lot after six hours of driving." It's the first and only time I've ever heard Sarah brag on me, and I kind of like it.

An hour later, the three of us are eating fish and chips at an outside table of a Main Street restaurant and Sarah and I are sipping thirty-year-old single-malts. At 9:45, the sun still clings to a corner of the sky. "I think Scotland is pretty terrific," I say.

"Me too," says Noah.

"It's wonderful," agrees Sarah, "and you've got to try to play a tournament while we're here."

"Really? This isn't supposed to be a golf trip."

"I know, but you've never played better and these conditions are tailor-made for your game." She drains the last of her whiskey and asks the waiter for two more. "You just shot a course record on a course you had never seen before without taking a single practice shot. And you spent the previous six hours behind the wheel. Call Finchem, he likes you. Explain the situation. Ask him for a favor. You've got nothing to lose."

"It's almost ten p.m."

"Which means it's five in Florida. He's not a slacker. Even on a Friday, he'll be there."

"And what do I ask for, exactly?"

"A sponsor's exemption into a European Senior event. You said there was one in Scotland this week. Come on. Don't overthink it. Just make the call."

Hesitantly, I pull out my phone. "It doesn't look like I have cell service."

She points at the anachronistic red pay phone directly across the street.

"Aren't you going to get sick of watching me play? I'm not always going to shoot sixty-ones."

"Walking a course here is nothing like in America. The terrain, the air, the feel of the ground. It's wonderful."

"And how about Noah?"

He doesn't look as enthused at the prospect as Sarah, but then again, he isn't on his second Scotch.

"Trust me, it will be good for Noah to see his father play and to see him play in Scotland. And although I'm a little embarrassed to say it, I forgot how much I love watching you play. It feels like being in college again."

I cross the street, push the hinged door shut behind me, and stare over at Sarah, who lifts her glass and smiles. An overseas operator charges the call to my home number and puts me through to Ponte Vedra.

"Tim, how are you? It's Travis McKinley."

"Travis.... you sound like you're calling from dark side of the moon. Where the hell are you?"

"Dornoch...in the Scottish Highlands."

"I know where it is, Travis. I've been there five times. I love that town."

"I can see why."

"So you're calling to check in and fill me in on your travels? How's Sarah?"

"Great. In fact, I'm calling at her request."

"Really?"

"You see, she and this guy named Andy, a plumber from Edinburgh...and Noah and Louie, our dog..."

"Travis, have you been drinking?"

"Of course I've been drinking. It's Scotland.... Yeah, so Sarah and Andy and Noah and Louie just saw me shoot a sixty-one at Royal Dornoch. Teed off at 6 p.m."

"The perfect time to play...and that's got to be close to a course record."

"It *is* the course record."

"Try not to lose the scorecard."

"I'm not calling to brag, although you should feel free to share the news with anyone you come into contact with. I'm calling because Sarah put me up to it. She thinks I'm in such rare form, I should try to play a tournament. I know you're a busy man, you've got other things to do, but she insisted I ask if you could get me a sponsor's exemption into the field at whatever Senior event they got going next week. Any chance of that?"

The other end goes silent and when I look up I see that Sarah is doing a little dance on the sidewalk. Noah is laughing and Louie looks alarmed.

"It's kind of late for that," says Finchem, finally. "I don't have many dealings with the European Seniors. Offhand, I wouldn't even know who to call. So I don't want to get your—or Sarah's—hopes up—but I'll see what I can do and call you back tomorrow at four o'clock."

"Cell service is spotty here. I'll give you my cell, but you should probably use this number," I say, and give him the number of the pay phone.

"Be by that phone tomorrow afternoon at four...and by the way, Travis, you're a lucky man."

"I know. No one shoots sixty-one without a little luck."

"I'm not talking about your round, Travis."

42

THE NEXT MORNING, SARAH, who is unaccustomed to three generous whiskeys at dinner, is not feeling too sprightly, and Noah and I brave the dining room of the Old Manse alone. A dozen diners are already there and as we enter the room and take a small table by the window, every one of them looks up and says, "Good morning." For both of us, it's our first stay at a B&B, and the unexpected intimacy with our fellow guests is a bit disconcerting, and we can't quite figure out why the fact that our shared roof is on a large house rather than a hotel makes such a difference.

"That's one of the reasons why you travel, Noah. To experience different things."

"I guess."

Breakfast is also different. In the Scottish version, it's a much more crowded plate — the fried eggs surrounded by baked beans, mushroom caps, cooked tomatoes. And there's a medley of meats that include their version of bacon, sausage, and several blackened discs which we are told are blood sausages.

"I think the breakfast is great," I say. "I love the sausage and beans and eggs all together."

"Beans for breakfast?" says Noah. "Sorry."

When we get upstairs, Sarah has pulled the sheets over her head. We grab Louie and walk into town and I'm relieved to see that the pay phone is still there. At the local grocery, we buy a muffin and a large bottle of water for Sarah along with a London *Times,* which bears the front-page headline ST. ANDREWS BRACES FOR TIGERMANIA, lay it all quietly on her night table, and set out exploring in the van. We end up in the fishing village of Portmahomack, where we buy lunch from a food truck and walk out to a lighthouse, described as the third tallest in Scotland.

We get back to Dornoch twenty minutes before Finchem is due to call, and take another walk through town, visiting its most significant nongolfing landmark, a thirteenth-century cathedral. When we loop back, the pay phone booth is occupied in every sense of the word by a teenage girl in a black leather motorcycle jacket. Her hair is bleached the same white as THE REZILLOS painted on the back of her jacket.

"Who are the Rezillos?" asks Noah.

"Never heard of them, but probably the name of her favorite band."

As it gets closer to four, the three of us edge nearer to the booth, but the conversation inside shows no sign of ebbing, and when I attempt a bit of universal mime—tapping my wrist with a finger and then holding my hand to my ear to convey I'm waiting on an important call, she responds with a universal gesture of her own.

"Dad, that girl just flipped you the bird."

"She did, didn't she?"

A quick glance at my watch confirms that the minute hand is straight up.

"Noah, we have no choice. We got to see her and raise her. With lots of attitude. And try to curl your lip as you do it. Ready?"

"I was born ready."

"On three. One...two..." On three, we come up with double barrels blazing, our faces twisted into snarls. A passerby would be less than impressed to see a father and son flipping off a teenage girl in a phone booth, but fortunately the street is empty and our target is the only witness.

Rather than being irked, the teen hoots audibly, replaces the phone, and steps out, our cause probably helped by the fact that we're both wearing Spinal Tap T-shirts. "It's all yours, gents."

Seconds later, the tower tolls and the phone rings.

"Travis, this is Tim. I couldn't get you into the Senior stop. Sorry, it was too late, but I twisted a couple of arms and called in a favor and got you into the Monday qualifier for the Scottish Open. The main event is at Loch Lomond, a new course that's supposed to be spectacular, and the qualifier is up the road a bit at North Berwick, so if nothing else you'll get a crack at another charming old Scottish links."

"Thanks, Tim, I'll try to make you proud."

"I'll settle for not being embarrassed.... Freedom and whiskey gang the gither! Take off your dram."

"Tim?"

"A toast, courtesy of the great Scottish poet Robert Burns. Good luck, Travis."

"What did he say?" asks Noah.

"Freedom and whiskey gang the gither! Take off your dram!"

43

TIM WAS RIGHT. THE West Links of North Berwick Golf Club, which was founded in 1832 and whose members have included the prime minister of Great Britain and Burt Lancaster, is a wildly entertaining layout, which reminds you on every hole that golf is a game, not a religion. There are blind shots and ditches and barely a straightforward level lie and greens whose precarious slopes funnel balls down to the rocky beach. Its signature is the ancient stone walls that weave through the course like a happy drunk. On multiple holes, the stonework has to be avoided, navigated, or hurdled, and on 16 a wall creeps onto the actual putting surface, so that a golfer might find himself having to take an unplayable from a green.

Then again, a course's eccentricities are a lot more beguiling when you're rolling in putts from hither and yon and bouncing a chip off the wall on 16 directly into the cup, miniature golf style, for your seventh birdie of the morning. "This is one charming golf course," I whisper to myself as I shamelessly pluck the ball from the hole and toss it to the gallery, all of whom are related to me, either through marriage, birth, or dog food. It's all the same to me, Royal Dornoch or North Berwick, as long as it's Scottish, ancient, and a links, and my 63 (there was also an eagle on 10) wins the qualifier going away.

That afternoon, we motor directly to Loch Lomond, a posh country club that attracts wealthy members from all over the world and whose parking lot is sprinkled with Bentleys and Aston Martins and Jaguars. Unbeknownst to me, the Scottish Open is always held the week before the Open Championship, and apparently many of the world's best golfers use it as their final tune-up, and as I walk the range with Sarah and Noah and Louie, I'm agog at the quality of the field. Side by side are Ernie Els, Retief Goosen, Phil Mickelson, Nick Faldo, and the twenty-year-old Spanish phenom Sergio García, who creates more lag on his irons than I've ever seen.

The next morning, I enlist Loch Lomond's fourteen-year-old club champion, Russell Knox, as my caddy, and he spends the next two days familiarizing me with the layout. Designed by Tom Weiskopf, the course flows gracefully through the riverside parkland and is breathtakingly beautiful. However, it's neither old, nor a links, nor distinctly Scottish, and as a result doesn't stir my kilt quite like Royal Dornoch or North Berwick, or tap into my newfound Scottish soul. And it doesn't have the same effect on my putter.

I'm still playing well, and having Sarah and Noah and Louie walking beside me keeps me on an even keel, but if I'm not dropping two or three field-goal-length putts a round it's hard to go crazy Dornochian low. Nevertheless, I shoot two subpar rounds and comfortably make the cut, no minor accomplishment at a regular European stop with such an elite field. I continue to play well on Saturday and early Sunday and I'm enjoying the prospect of a payday fat enough to cover the cost of the courtesy van, if not the whole trip. A strong front nine moves me into the top twenty. When I reach the 18th green, my novice caddy makes the mistake of informing me that if I could finish with a birdie, the field is so strong and filled with so many golfers who have already qualified, it might be enough to get me one of the last four invitations to the Open Championship.

That was more than I needed to know at that moment, and with images of St. Andrews dancing in my brain, I yank the eighteen-foot putt three feet left.

It turns out my caddy's hunch was dead-on and my two-putt par leaves me in fourteenth place, one place short of St. Andrews.

44

It's disappointing to have narrowly missed a chance to tee it up in a major, but the biggest check I've cashed in three years eases the sting. So does the satisfaction of a top fifteen in an elite European event. All I want to do right now is kick back and celebrate, dip into my winnings, and share it with my merry band of travelers. Even as we sit outside the scorers' tent, my fourteenth-place money is burning a hole in my pocket.

"How about we get off the road for a few days and live large?"

"What do you have in mind?" asks Sarah.

"A castle."

"That works."

Castle hotels are, in fact, a category of accommodation in Scotland, and the nearest one that offers the level of service I have in mind—"Don't show me anything less than five stars," I tell Sarah—is Inverlochy Castle near Torlundy and Fort William, about three hours away. A nasal voice at the end of the line informs me that Inverlochy is pleased to offer suites and deluxe suites and adjoining deluxe suites and for the even more discriminating guest, something called the Gate Lodge, which is a separate free-standing structure, a little castle of its own. The Gate Lodge comes with everything except a moat, and when she assures me it should be more than adequate for a couple, one child, and a small dog, I book it immediately, before some other fool with more money than sense grabs it out from under us.

We check in that afternoon and it doesn't disappoint. Over the next couple of days, we take in the occasional site like the falls at Glen Nevis and the monument at Glenfinnan, but mainly we just pad around the old pile in our bathrobes and slippers and luxuriate in the Egyptian 400-thread-count bed linens and the full breadth of Arran aromatic toiletries. And when that gets old, Noah changes the combination on our personal safe. Although we've taken to calling ourselves Sir Travis, Lady Sarah, and Prince Noah, our real role models are the Clampetts, as in Jed, not Bobby.

Wednesday afternoon, I call in a room service lunch of Scottish smoked salmon and champagne and park myself in front of the forty-inch TV. They're replaying the final round of the '95 Open, the event won by John Daly the last time it was contested on the Old Course.

"He doesn't give a toss," said Andy of Daly at Dornoch. He's right. Daly couldn't hit his driver like that on 18 if he did. I've never had the luxury of not giving a toss, don't even know what it would be like. Maybe it would feel a little like this robe and slippers. And taste a little like this salmon reeled from a local loch. I pull the robe a little snugger and take another bite of smoked fish.

As I do, I try to ignore the chirping cell phone on the couch. The number is Scottish. Who in Scotland has my number? No one I can think of. I reach for the phone and keep chewing.

"Good afternoon, this is Angus Farquhar, assistant secretary of the R&A."

"Excuse me?"

"The R&A. The Royal and Ancient Golf Club of St. Andrews. Is this Travis McKinley?" On the screen, Daly lines up his final putt on 18, the great stone clubhouse of the R&A rearing up behind the green. So, although it's five years later, I'm looking at the building from which Angus is calling.

"Travis, have I caught you at a bad time?"

"Not really."

"I got your number from Tim Finchem and have news that could be of interest. Alex Jeffers, who finished just ahead of you at Loch Lomond, has had a crisis of con-science. He thinks there may have been a double hit on his chip on the tenth hole Friday afternoon at Loch Lomond, and has given up his spot for the Open Cham-pionship. You are next in line." *Kind of like an heir to the throne, I think. Sort of like Prince Noah.* "That means his exemption is yours, that is, if you want it and can get to St. Andrews in time to tee off at seven-oh-three tomorrow morning."

"Angus, can I put you on hold for thirty seconds?"

I turn to Lady Sarah and Prince Noah, both of whom are also still in their robes, and explain that I have just been offered the last spot in the Open Championship, maybe some kind of trickle-down karma from Tucson. The bad news is that if I accept it, we will have to leave all this behind. Immediately. What should I do?

45

WE ATTEND TO THE little details required when you decide to pry yourself from the lap of luxury. We settle our prodigious bill and duke the maids. We repack the van, finding places to stuff the bathrobes and all those little tubes of body wash and shampoo, and pack a last supper picnic of Scottish salmon and rye. It's 6 p.m. by the time we're back on the road.

Ahead of us are 135 miles on the A9, and in our excitement it takes nearly an hour for it to dawn on us that we don't have a place to stay. Thankfully, we have cell service, and Sarah starts making calls on my phone. We're not expecting to duplicate the Gate Lodge or those Egyptian linens, and no one can stop us from enjoying our bathrobes, which, by the way, we paid for, but it soon becomes clear that finding a hotel room within 100 miles of St. Andrews the day before the Open Championship is impossible. Everything has been booked for months. "You must be dreaming," a receptionist tells Sarah.

"No problem," I say. "We'll sleep in the courtesy van." Unfortunately, it's the same story with campsites. Finding a spot in an empty field is no easier than getting into the field of the championship itself. There are no last-minute crises of conscience among the thousands of arriving golf fans, and when we pull off the motorway the issue remains unresolved.

St. Andrews is a charming seaside town that seems far more substantial than its population of 16,000. We pass the border of the Old Course and eye the formidable clubhouse of the Royal and Ancient Golf Club, which looks out not just over the Old Course but over the sport itself. I cruise up and down Scores, Market, and North Streets, searching in vain for a space big enough to park a large ambulance.

After a fruitless half hour, it becomes clear that some creative trespassing may be required, and having successfully snuck onto Augusta National, it's a pocket of low-level criminality at which I have some expertise and maybe even a little talent. It's a matter of being attuned to the main chance, and I try to stay positive as we inch along the crowded streets past the packed pubs and overbooked hotels, past the old movie house and the cathedral and down to the harbor. In addition to the golf course, the town is home to the University of St. Andrews, also one of the oldest in the world, and as we circle back from the harbor we find ourselves on a street lined with university offices. On our right, a stately private residence has been converted into the home of its economics department.

"I've always been curious about the St. Andrews School of Economics," I say, and turn through the impressive gate.

"Really?" says Sarah. "You've never expressed it before."

"I know. I'm funny that way."

"What aspect of the school are you curious about?"

"Lots of things, but particularly their parking."

In back of the building are two rows of cars, presumably belonging to distinguished faculty, and I discreetly squeeze our large white vehicle in among them.

"Doesn't stand out too much," says Sarah.

"You know the motto of St. Andrews School of Economics?"

"No."

"It's in Latin, but the approximate English translation is 'Money talks and bullshit walks.'"

"You're feeling pretty good about yourself, aren't you, Sir Travis?"

"If you're going to tee it up in the Open you better be," I say. "But there's still some work to be done. While you three get settled, I'm going to walk over to the R&A."

I head out the driveway and up the street. Just over the

hill is the course and to the right a row of small hotels. I poke my head into the nearest and ask a waitress if there is a pub frequented by caddies.

"What pub isn't frequented by caddies? But I'd start with Dunvegan...just around the corner."

At a little past ten, Dunvegan, unlike its neighbors, shows no signs of slowing down. I take a seat at the crowded bar and order a Tennent. My last-minute invite has me feeling both euphoric and overwhelmed and I sip my Tennent and gather my thoughts. My tee time is nine hours away and I still don't have a caddy. And based on everything I've read, no track requires more local knowledge.

As I survey the room, trying to determine who looks approachable and who stands a chance of sobering up in time, a man about my age taps me on the shoulder and says, "Travis, I can't believe you actually listened."

It takes me a second to recognize him with his clothes on. It's my neighbor from the driving range in Encino.

"Seamus! Great to see you. You've been on my mind more than you might think. But what the hell are you talking about?"

"I said you had to go back to the beginning and here you are in St. Andrews, where it all began."

"So that's what you meant. I wasted months on that riddle."

"Before we go any further," says Seamus, "congrats on Loch Lomond. To finish in the money in that company you got to be golfing your ball. I take it you've come down the road to watch?"

"No...to play. Based on my fourteenth-place finish, I was the next alternate and it opened up this afternoon. And I need a caddy. Do you know the course?"

"I've been coming here for twenty-five years. I know it like the back of my hand."

Would that be your left or right? I think. But I hold my tongue and arrange to meet him at dawn.

"Before you head off to sleep," says Seamus, "do one thing for me. Sit on the stool like this facing the room and watch the TV behind the bar by looking back at it over your shoulder, first over your left for about thirty seconds and then your right. Back and forth ten times each. Best thing you can do for your ROM—range of motion."

46

MY FIRST REACTION TO the course is "Where is it?" From the tee box, I face a gray expanse as featureless as a Walmart parking lot. There don't seem to be any holes. Last night in the van, I perused the layout and gave myself a crash course on its eccentricities—the seven double greens with white flags for the outward holes and red for the inward, the 120 bunkers, all of which have names and some of which are located in the middle of fairways. In person, the holes have much less definition than on the card. With no trees, it's impossible to make out the fairways, and with no fairways, there's no clear idea of where to aim.

On the range, I introduced Seamus to Sarah and Noah and Louie. Then I gave Seamus the distances I hit my clubs and he laid out our game plan. "I'm going to give you a club and a target and unless I specify differently, you're going to put your smoothest eighty-five-percent swing on it. Then we're going to go find it and do it again. Other than that, you're just along to absorb the atmosphere and take in the sights."

The tee shot on No. 1 is almost absurdly easy. It's a short hole, 376 yards, and you have two fairways to hit into—1 and 18—and between them they are 130 yards wide. Seamus pulls my hybrid 3 and points left at a lone gorse in the center of a featureless field. Last night, as I crammed for this test, I searched out the worst of the trouble, the places you least want to visit. Except for the armada of bunkers, it's all to the right. The stern warning I gave myself that first morning in England as we pulled out of the parking lot in our rental—*RIGHT equals DEATH*—is as applicable to the Old Course as the M6. Swerve right, you're roadkill. Keep it left, you're pretty much in every hole. This is no course for old men...who are fighting a slice...but for a middle-aged fellow like myself, whose go-to shot is a low hard hook, it's quite hospitable.

Speaking of right, I glance in that direction. Sarah, who looks damn good for 7 a.m., smiles and waves, and Noah, who shows no indication of ever getting out from under *This Is Spinal Tap,* raises his pinkie and pointer finger in the international sign of rock 'n' roll solidarity. At least he doesn't curl his lip and flip me the bird.

Sarah and Noah are easy to spot. I'm going off in the third pairing of the day with Kazuhiko Hosokawa and Tsuyoshi Yoneyama, and Sarah and Noah are the only Caucasian faces in a small sea of ardent Japanese fans. Many of the women carry open umbrellas against the invisible Scottish sun.

My hybrid flies about 215 yards and rolls another 50, leaving me 123 to the pin. The only thing challenging about the shot, along with the circumstances, is the Swilcan Burn, a piddling irrigation ditch of a stream that runs directly in front of the green on its way to the sea. It's maybe six feet wide and a foot deep but catches so many balls they leave a metal scooper beside it to pluck them out. My wedge barely clears the burn, but the greens are so hard and fast the ball still rolls twenty feet past the hole. I find the contours of the greens as nebulous as the fairways and am entirely in Seamus's hands. "Twenty feet that plays like twelve," he says, "two balls to the right." His read is spot-on and so is my putt and when it finds the hole my constituency erupts.

"How does it feel?" asks Seamus as we step over to the No. 2.

"How does what feel?"

"To be the leader of the Open Championship? And please don't say it's humbling."

47

IT MUST FEEL GOOD, because I birdie the second and third as well, two more indistinguishable par 4s, and as I step onto the fourth tee, my mind is focused. My only concern is that the raw data of my birdie, birdie, birdie start has been collected and transmitted to the keepers of the large electronic scoreboards scattered over the course, and that no one else has matched my start.

That's not exactly true. I hope for one other thing as well, which is that out of the thousands of golf fans already milling about the grounds, one of them will have a sufficiently developed sense of the absurd to snap a picture of a leaderboard, and later reach out so that he or she can get me the photo. Back in Winnetka, I'll frame and display it as irrefutable proof that one cool gray morning in the mists of time, a McKinley, Travis to be more precise, gazed out from fairway to firth, master of all he surveyed. I'm not planning on anything gaudy or ostentatious, just a simple black frame with a matte white background and maybe some recessed spotlighting, and I wouldn't put it up in more than three or four rooms. Also, I would have a lot more parties.

Once in wish list mode, it's hard to snap out of it, because as soon as I conceive my hope for an enterprising imaginative photographer, I layer on another wish, my third, which is that the players just below me on the leaderboard will not be as anonymous or Asian as Hosokawa and Yoneyama, but iconic names known throughout the Western world like Faldo and Watson and Woods, to give my moment some context.

Perhaps you've already concluded that these kinds of thoughts, and I use the word charitably, are the least appropriate for someone contending with 156 of the best golfers in the world, and almost as many hungry bunkers, with annoyingly picturesque names like Pulpit and Principal's Nose. If so, you'd be wrong. Rather than the standard pitfall, which is to get ahead of yourself and start fantasizing about your new status and life if by some miracle you are able to keep this up and hoist the Claret Jug, I'm staying well behind myself and focusing entirely on what I've already done, how it might be recorded for posterity and expressed as interior decorating. And it turns out to be quite helpful. Although I don't record any more birdies, I don't post a single bogey, either, and at the end of the day my 69 is good enough for a share of the lead along with half a dozen other golfers, all of whom I'm happy to be associated with, including Ernie Els and Pádraig Harrington. And later that afternoon before Sarah, Noah, and Louie join me for a walk around the gray old town, a friendly stranger snaps a few pictures of the leaderboard with the four of us and Seamus standing in front of it and promises to send me the pictures.

So I'm good to go.

48

FRIDAY AFTERNOON, SEAMUS ASKS me to meet him at the Martyrs' Monument, a tall, austere piece of commemorative granite that sits on a bluff and looks over the back of the Royal and Ancient Golf Club and the epic sweep of the beach. Seamus is waiting on a nearby bench with my clubs and a small stack of British tabloids, all of whose headlines refer to me—EX-BROADCASTER LEADS OPEN . . . AMERICAN SENIOR CLAIMS PIECE OF LEAD . . . MCKINLEY WHO?

"I'd like to perform a cleansing ritual," he says, and pats the empty spot beside him.

"Knock yourself out."

"Please close your eyes," he says, "and inhale deeply. Hold it for a beat. Now release the breath through your nose. Feel the sun on your face and the breeze off the sea. Smell the brine. Be the brine."

I'm okay with "be the ball," but be the brine?

"Listen to the birds…and the waves. I know this all seems unreal, Travis—coming in late last night and leading the Open Championship. And you're right, it isn't real. It's completely unreal. But the thing to keep in mind is that so is everything else. This bench. This obelisk. It's all an illusion. In a couple hundred years, maybe less, this entire course will be under water and all that will be left are the birds and waves and sun and maybe the tip of that obelisk, and no one will care who led the Open Championship after the first round or second or even whose names are engraved on the Claret Jug. So none of this really matters. Do you understand that?"

"Kind of."

"Do you believe it?"

"No."

"Neither do I. Let's just bag this experiment and go golfing."

On Friday, the group of Hosokawa, Yoneyama, and McKinley goes off at 4:52 p.m. and I get a second look at the Old Course. Although both are hundreds of years old, overlook the North Sea, and are built on the edge of charming Scottish towns, the Old Course and Royal Dornoch could not be more different. Dornoch feels like a discovery, that you're planting a flag on new golfing land. At St. Andrews, pronounced "Sin*and*rooze," there's no mistaking you've stepped onto the most golfed

track on earth. It's the muni of all munis. People have
been playing it for six hundred years and it looks it.
Even on a sunny day you feel like you're seeing it in
black-and-white, and, like all the most revered munis,
it feels chilly to outsiders. It reminds me of a legendary
inner-city playground where the greatest athletes have
done battle for generations and there are no nets on the
rims. And yet somehow it's not played out. Not even
close.

For the second day in a row, Seamus guides me through
the peril like a Seeing Eye dog. Most critical is avoiding
the deep bunkers strewn over the turf like land mines, and
somehow we do. And my ground hook continues to serve
me well. It swerves away from the trouble on the right
and rolls forever on these firm fairways, so my disadvantage off the tee, compared to the youngs, is minimized
and on most holes, I'm hitting the same irons and wedges
into the greens as players twenty years my junior. And despite my deficiencies as a putter, I'm as comfortable on
these greens as at Dornoch and North Berwick. On a U.S.
Open layout, I'd be lucky to break 80, but here, at least so
far, I'm competitive.

I don't get off to the same hellacious start as Thursday,
but I keep my nose and card clean and, based on three
birdies in a five-hole stretch in the middle of the round,
put up another 69 and cling to a piece of the lead along

with Thomas Bjørn, Colin Montgomerie, and a golfer you may be familiar with named Tiger Woods.

Just off 18, Sarah, Noah, and Louie give us a royal reception. "Amazing," says Sarah, hugging us both. "You two are kicking ass and taking names."

"Not only that," says Noah, "you're going to be huge in Japan."

I'm just thrilled to have made another cut, and after Seamus retires for the evening I explain to Sarah that even if I finish last, which I still consider likely, I'm guaranteed £10,999, which according to the calculator on my phone is worth $16,697.11. "Half the field just got sent home and eighty hotel rooms opened up. So let's ixnay the van and check into another luxury suite. I miss those four-hundred-thread-count sheets and down comforters. Life is short, and according to Seamus, none of it is real anyway. It's all just an illusion."

"What are you talking about?" says Sarah. "And there's no way we're moving now and messing with your karma. Are you crazy?"

And so we faithfully adhere to our little routine. After everyone but Louie takes advantage of my player's credential to shower—Noah and I at the R&A and Sarah at the nearby Forgan House—we enjoy fish and chips at our regular, then stroll the town in the lingering light. St. Andrews, the town, is as warm and welcoming as the course is not, and townspeople smile and doff their hats as we wend our way from the antique-looking picture house on Market Street past the genuinely ancient cathedral and on down to the small harbor, where we have already found a little place that puts together a pretty fair ice cream cone. Just like home, we join the queue, pay up, and ferry our perishables to an empty table.

Postdessert, we resume our walk, circling back along the esplanade that runs behind the cathedral. When Louie barks, we notice that half a dozen Fleet Street photographers are shadowing us from across the street.

"I don't mind the pictures," I say, "but if they see the van we'll never hear the end of it."

"What are we going to do?" says Sarah. "You need some sleep."

"I have an idea . . . it's going to be a bit of an adventure."

"Cool," says Noah.

Next to the St. Andrews School of Economics is a bed-and-breakfast, and we turn off the sidewalk and walk to the door. "It's got to be unlocked," I say, "because they never know when their last guest will arrive or return for the evening. We'll go in the front and step out the back."

"Travis, at what point did you become an operative for the CIA? We could all get arrested. That would make a lovely headline—'Leader of Open Championship Deported for Breaking and Entering.'"

"Unlikely."

The photo corps have crossed the street and are setting up tripods by the gate. "The time has come to act," I say. "Freedom and whiskey gang the gither! Take off your dram."

"What?"

"Robert Burns," says Noah.

I grab the handle and the front door opens with a creak worthy of *The Addams Family* and Sarah and Noah succumb to giggling. Fortunately, no one hears them and we tiptoe through a pitch-black living room into the kitchen and out a side door. Minutes later, we slip unseen through a tall hedge and into the parking lot where our trusty white van awaits in the moonlight.

"Worked like a charm," says Noah.

"I'm on a roll, what can I say? And Noah, you should never try this on your own unless you're being hounded by paparazzi in a quaint Scottish town. Are we clear on that?"

"Dad, I don't think you're going to do much more rolling."

Slapped on every window of the van are aggressively adhesive NO TRESPASSING stickers, and bolted to the back wheel is a yellow rectangular encumbrance that resembles a medieval instrument of torture. "Just as I feared," I say, "the dreaded Sinandrooze boot."

49

DESPITE THE PAPERWORK AND impediment and our slippery legal footing, I sleep soundly on the lead for the second day in a row and so does the rest of the carhold, including Louie, who barely acknowledges the fact that his best friend is the thirty-six-hole leader of the Open Championship. Throughout the night, a brisk breeze ventilates our little dorm and rocks it like a cradle, but by 6 a.m., when the first light is visible through the thickets, the lullaby has turned into a tempest. From inside I can hear the wind trying to claw the stickers off the windows, and it's so fierce I'm almost grateful for the extra ballast on our back tire.

When I tug Louie out of bed for his morning constitutional the wind plasters his coat to his body like a bad toupee. The two of us lean into it and head up to the course to get an idea of what I will be facing. Without trees, the visible evidence is limited to the flapping flag on No. 18 and the heaving gorse along the right side of the fairway, but there is no doubt it's blowing a gale. Although I haven't read the play, or at least the CliffsNotes, since high school, the turbulent scene makes me think of old King Lear and how thoroughly he screwed up his life. I fear that when I go onstage, I'll screw up as tragically and be one more old man stumbling blindly across a windswept heath.

A few hours later, Seamus and I rendezvous at our favorite obelisk.

"You're not going to attempt another cleansing ritual, are you?"

"Strictly for amateurs. I got something much better in mind."

He shoulders my bag and we head down the hill. He sidesteps the range and keeps going until we reach the entrance to Jubilee, a newer course that runs adjacent to the Old Course, and continues past the closed pro shop. "I'm taking you someplace special. A place only locals know."

We take the path that runs beside the first two fairways and just before the third, tack left into a large open area where there are three heaping piles of sand and gravel and dozens of trucks and pieces of earth-moving machinery, in various states of repair. Beyond it to the right is a practice area with a green and a bunker and enough space to hit full wedges. The cul-de-sac is shielded from view and the elements by a large dune, and although we can hear the wind whipping across the waves, I feel utterly cut off from the fray.

A hundred yards from the green, Seamus lowers my bag and empties a plastic tube of balls at my feet and for the next ninety minutes, it's just the two of us, out of sight and out of the wind, hitting and shagging balls.

"I want you to find a spot as tranquil as this inside yourself," says Seamus. "Before every shot and every putt I want you to get really quiet. Whatever you're feeling, I need you to lower the volume, take a breath, and lower it some more. It's going to get hairy as hell out there, and I want your mind and body to be a source of comfort, not something you fight. It should be a refuge, a sanctuary, like this spot here, where no one can mess with us. It might be a little Zen for your taste, but try to buy into it. It will help."

For Saturday, groups are trimmed from three to two, and I go out second-to-last with Danish pro Thomas Bjørn. Although little known in America, he has a dozen wins in Europe and played in a Ryder Cup. He's big and strong and known for his dark gloomy demeanor— Hamlet to my Lear.

When I step on the first tee, an enormous gallery is standing six and seven deep from the steps of the R&A

to the corner of Market Street. Only a handful are Asian. Mostly they are locals, attracted by my Scottish name and heritage and the unlikelihood of a fifty-four-year-old not good enough to keep his card on the Senior Tour bidding to win the oldest and grandest major of them all. In barely decipherable brogues, they urge me to dig deep and represent. "Let's go, laddie!" "Come on, McKinley!" "Don't lose your nerve, boyo!" "One more time for us old bastards!"

There must be three thousand people packed behind the tee, and I have just enough time to locate my bunkmates. Overhead the sky glowers like Armageddon and the strength of the cold wind is terrifying. The wind and cold remind me of the dread I felt every morning as an eight-year-old at YMCA camp before being forced into the freezing lake whose Native American name I have thankfully forgotten. But when a gust blows a tweed cap off the scalp of a tournament volunteer and sends it bounding down the fairway like a jackrabbit, I experience a sudden adjustment in attitude and point of view. You might even call it an epiphany.

Generally harsh conditions will separate the wheat from the chaff, but when it gets ridiculous and crosses over the line, it does the opposite. Unplayable is unplayable, whether you're Thomas Bjørn or Travis McKinley or even Tiger Woods. The wind, I realize, will level the playing field, and as the worst golfer among the leaders, if not the entire field, any leveling favors me most of all.

My ball flight is already low. I move the ball back in my stance, and I hit it even lower, like an intentional top. It doesn't go fifteen feet off the ground but has an enormous amount of top spin, and on my first several drives it rolls twenty yards past the much younger and stronger Bjørn, making him an even more melancholy Dane. I open with five consecutive pars. When I get my first glimpse of the leaderboard at the 6th tee, I see that that's enough to put me alone in first, and when I par the next four, my lead swells to three strokes.

I bogey 10, 11, and 12 but stay safely tucked inside my head as if in that becalmed space behind the dunes. On the next leaderboard, I see that my rivals did worse and my lead has stretched to four. I par out for 75, the best round of the day so far, and my lead is up to five strokes. Tied for second are Tiger Woods and Tom Lehman, who are just finishing on 18.

As I huddle with Seamus and try to digest the reality, a British reporter sticks his microphone in my face and asks who I would rather be paired with, Lehman or Woods? The reporter is about my age, and I recall my own short-lived attempt at on-course reporting, and how difficult it was to get golfers to say something/anything.

"I want to be paired with Tiger," I say. "No disrespect

to Tom or anyone else, but if I'm going to choke my brains out, I want to do it in front of the best golfer who ever lived."

As I blather on like a candid fool, Tiger pours a twelve-footer dead center and punches his ticket for the final group. I think of something my mother used to say. "Be careful what you wish for, Travis. You just might get it."

50

LATE SUNDAY MORNING, I get a call from Seamus. "Same time, same place" is all he says. By 2:30, the two of us are sitting on our usual bench by the monument sipping our coffee and gazing off into the horizon like a pair of pensioners.

"Beautiful day," I say morosely.

"Tell me about it."

With the wind gone, the last round will be a test of skill, not survival, which is unlikely to favor yours truly. "So where you taking me today?"

He points at the water, takes two last gulps, and tosses the empty cup in the trash. I do the same and follow him down off the bluff, across the putting green, and down the cement stairs to the beach. A wet breeze is blowing in off the whitecaps, and gulls circle overhead.

"Remember that opening scene from *Chariots of Fire?*

Of course you do. All those pale overbred British types in retro activewear sprinting barefoot on the sand. They're running at the waterline where the sand is nice and packed and sometimes the waves wash over their feet and that great soundtrack by Vangelis swells up under it. Something about the combination of that music with those images makes you bawl—it's pretty much auto-matic.

"That scene, that opening sequence from the movie, was shot right here where we're standing now on West Sands, and I can't think of a more appropriate place to share my last bits of wisdom and inspiration before we head out for the last round of the Open Championship. You know what, humor me, let's take our shoes off so we can really get into the spirit of the scene. We don't have to get our feet wet, just walk barefoot for a while."

I don't want to seem like a bad sport. Seamus has ob-viously gone to a lot of effort to come up with the right message and delivery. One side at a time, I pull off my shoes and socks and stuff the socks in the shoes, and it's harder than you might think while standing on one foot. Also, the sand feels a lot colder when you're not sprint-ing and the blood isn't flowing and you're fifty-four and haven't run for anything but a cab in twenty years.

"All night and morning," says Seamus, "I've been think-ing of what to tell you. The best way to send you out into battle. At the same time, I want to keep it simple so there are not too many ideas bouncing around in your head. Six hours from now, a golfer will win this tournament. He will thank the R&A and the sponsors for putting on the best tournament in the world and raise the Claret Jug, which comes with the designation 'Champion Golfer of the Year,' which you got to admit has a pretty nice ring to it. Then he will put his lips to it and turn to one side and then the other so the photographers on both sides can get that shot of him kissing the trophy in profile.

"The most important thing, which you've got to realize and keep in mind all day, is that golfer is not going to be you. There is no way a fifty-four-year-old journeyman refugee from the Senior Tour is going to hold off Tiger for eighteen holes on Sunday to win a major. The universe and Tiger Woods are not going to let that happen. It's a nonstarter."

I had to take off my shoes and socks and prance around in the freezing sand for this? Somewhere on Ibiza, Evangelos Odysseas Papathanassiou, aka Vangelis, is puking into the Mediterranean.

"Travis, you're not going to win this tournament. There's no way at the end of this round that Sarah and Noah and Louie are going to come racing out onto the eighteenth green. By the way, wives and children should not be encouraged to run out onto the course. Who the hell came up with that one? Golf is not about family. It's about golf and that's plenty. If anything, it's about getting away from your family for a few hours. Maybe that's why the wives and children are so excited when they get out there on the green. They haven't seen the guy in so long. 'Johnny, that's Daddy, remember him?' . . . 'Kind of.' In any case, unless Tiger has a wife and kids no one knows about, I assure you, the eighteenth green is going to be a wife-, child-, and dog-free zone.

"Last night, as you lay in bed, did you hoist the jug in your dreams? No. Well, it's not going to happen in real life, either. So relax. Enjoy every last minute of this round, of playing in the last group on the oldest course in the world where the game was invented by some bored shepherd. No matter what happens today, Travis McKinley will be part of golfing history. You are a golfer, a damn good one, and you are part of this wonderful mostly male tradition of people who have pissed away the better part of their lives trying to develop a repeatable golf swing."

Six hundred years is a long time and no doubt there have been a lot of lackluster pep talks delivered by caddies to golfers over that span, but I can safely say this has to be the worst ever. Not only is it depressing, it's tedious and goes on forever.

Or maybe it's the best and one day they will teach it at Harvard Business School. And maybe Seamus, bless his schizoid soul, is a stone-cold genius, a natural-born leader of men in Softspikes, and like Vince Lombardi, they will name a service area after him on the New Jersey Turnpike. Because ninety minutes later, when the starter clears his throat and announces the arrival on the tee of the final pairing of the day, starting with "The U.S. Open Champion Tiger Woods from Windermere, Florida," and soon after, through the same public-address system and brogue, utters the words "Travis McKinley from Winnetka, Illinois," and I step on the tee in front of six thousand spectators, I discover that I can walk and breathe at the same time.

And when I stick my tee into the hallowed turf, my hand shakes so slightly that my Pro V1x doesn't topple off and cause several hundred people to snicker. No, it stays right up there on the tee where I put it. And as I take my last practice swings, I find that I can also breathe and swing at the same time. Not only that, I can concentrate. Instead of thirty things I shouldn't be thinking about, I'm just thinking target and tempo, like at the back range at Creekview Country Club.

As a result, I don't whiff or top it, or produce the shot whose name can never be spoken aloud that begins with *s* and ends with *k* but flush it dead center. The ball flies straight at the gorse bush by the burn like it has the three days before and with a wink at Sarah and a nod at Noah, we're off.

51

Dressed in his conquistadorial Sunday red and black, Tiger struts off the first tee as if he's the one sitting on a five-stroke cushion, instead of me, and Seamus and I chase after him. My opening salvo, a hybrid-3, stopped five yards short of Tiger's 5-iron.

"Ninety-eight yards to carry the burn, one hundred and five to the flag," says Seamus, and along with my fifty-four-degree wedge, he repeats the same unequivocal vote of no confidence he delivered with such brio on the sands. "Travis, you are not going to win this tournament. Got that?"

"Got it."

"Good. Then put a nice little swing on this puppy, drop it somewhere on the dance floor, and see if we can't two-putt."

As you probably know, a five-stroke lead on the Old

Course is nothing. With these blustery winds and Daytona-esque greens and the title of Champion Golfer of the Year up for grabs, that kind of lead can vanish in a heartbeat. They're like crumbs from a crumpet on a picnic table in a hurricane. Which is why I'm grateful that I follow the first part of Seamus's directions and ignore the second, and when I roll in my eighteen-footer for birdie and Tiger lips out his five-footer for par, the two-shot swing fattens my lead to a more robust seven strokes.

Not that a couple of measly insurance strokes means Bo Diddley to Seamus. "You're not going to win this," he repeats with a patronizing smile as if that birdie/bogey exchange didn't happen, and for the next two hours he never veers off message. Sometimes he breaks the bad news with a shake of his head. At others with a Brooklynese "fuhgeddaboutit," and if he senses for even a minute that despite his drumbeat of negativity, I'm starting to daydream about a vessel used to hold red wine or hosting delusions that maybe, just maybe, this could be my lucky day, God forbid, he lays a hand on my shoulder like the Grim Reaper and says, "Read my lips—will...not...happen," and then he hands me whatever club is called for, whether driver, wedge, or knockdown 8, and says, "Now put some smooth on it."

When I make the turn in thirty-three and Tiger in thirty-seven, I've nursed and nurtured my lead to nine strokes, but Seamus has been so vigilant that my expectations are no more unrealistic than when I pulled into the parking lot of the St. Andrews School of Economics Wednesday evening and found that perfect only slightly illegal parking space. Nevertheless, it's difficult to be entirely immune to the knowledge that I'm sitting on nearly a two-digit margin with nine holes to go and unlike the Great Wallenda, I'm working with a net. In such rarefied air, I don't have the strength of character to resist a moment of eye contact with my old TV antagonist and Tiger's caddy, Steve Williams.

Williams, I am pleased to report, is not taking this well. In his carriage and expression, he barely resembles the man who came marching up the fairway four months ago to threaten me with bodily harm. On the contrary. His face is pained and paled and his lips are pursed, and he looks like someone with a highly inflamed hemorrhoid who has just shoved a microphone up his own ass. Unfortunately, on the back nine of a major on Sunday, these little indulgences don't come for free and this one results in my first lousy swing and bogey of the day. As we make our way to No. 11, my lead has been whittled to eight strokes.

Oh, well.

52

ALTHOUGH ONLY 174 YARDS, the No. 11 has earned its reputation as one of the most diabolical threes in the world. It's the steep tilt of the green from back to front, and the way the Hill and Strath bunkers guard the front, and the sickening regularity with which even well-struck irons can trickle off the putting surface into one or the other.

For the first time all day, Tiger has honors, and it's actually a disadvantage. The elevated green backs onto the Eden Estuary, and in the short time it takes to walk from the 10th to 11, the temperature has dropped ten degrees and the wind, manageable till now, has freshened dramatically. It blows straight off the water into our faces with gusts up to forty miles an hour. Out of respect for its strength, Tiger pulls 6, a club he normally hits 220 yards. Perhaps it's that little bit of momentum he picked up on

No. 10, or his sense that this is a hole with possibilities, because his swing is as solid as any I've witnessed at close range. It looks like Iron Byron with a crimson sweater and produces a low hard fade that shrugs off the elements with disdain.

For 172 yards, it augers through the wind like a motorized machine with a propeller behind it. At the tail end of its flight, however, as the ball loses speed, the wall of wind knocks it down, and instead of dropping in the middle of the green and working right toward the hole, it lands closer to the front. For an instant it stays put. Then wind and geography and gravity take over and the ball rolls back, spills over the edge, and dribbles into Strath bunker.

To see how shabbily the wind and slope treated Tiger is sobering. If Tiger's pured 6 wasn't enough, what do I need? A 4-iron? A 5-wood? An army surplus howitzer endorsed by the NRA? Apparently, it's even more sobering to Seamus, because he places his palm on the head of my putter.

"A bit soon for that, don't you think?"

"Nope. I want you to roll it. You saw what the wind did to Tiger's shot?"

"Unfortunately. I tried to avert my eyes but it was too late."

"So I don't have to tell you how well he hit that. Hogan couldn't have hit a better six in his dreams. We don't want to be right next to him in that bunker." He pulls out his yardage book and studies a drawing of the hole. "I want you to aim just right of Hill bunker, the one on the left, and let the ground slice do the rest. It should leave you just short of the green between the two bunkers."

"Seamus, you're embarrassing me. I have an eight-stroke lead and I'm hitting putter off the tee? In case you've forgotten, this is televised. Simon is watching with his girlfriend and my pals are watching at home. And so are my former colleagues at CBS."

"Travis, last time I checked you were a professional golfer. Worrying about what anyone else thinks is for amateurs. Besides, this is links golf," and then in his best imitation brogue, "It's Sinandrooze. Not some dog track in Hialeah. I want this ball shipped by UPS via standard ground delivery. And have fun with it."

Seamus pulls the putter and when the gallery realizes what he has just handed me, the volume of murmuring forces him to wave his arms for quiet. I can handle the murmuring. It's the snickering that pisses me off. And as I take my practice swings, or practice strokes, whichever you prefer, I feel like I'm standing up for Seamus as much as myself. Barely turning my shoulders, I beat down on the ball with my wrists. Somehow I strike it solid and the ball skitters down the hard fairway. By the time it approaches Hill, the murmuring and snickering have been replaced by rapt silence, and when, as Seamus predicted, the slope kicks it right, by thunderous applause. When it rolls up the bank and onto the green and stops eighteen feet above the hole, the crowd goes apeshit.

"Still feeling embarrassed?" asks Seamus.

"No, just blushing."

"Good, because they're going to be running that on ESPN for as long as there is life on earth."

53

WHILE THE BEDLAM SUBSIDES, Tiger studies the putting surface for the best place to land his bunker shot, then retreats down the slope like a miner trudging off to work. First his sweater drops from view and then his Nike cap, and I don't see anything until the glint at the top of his backswing. An instant later, there's an emphatic thump and a spray of sand and the ball rises straight up out of the bunker as if levitated. It lands on the spot Tiger had stared at, rolls uphill ten feet, and drops into the hole for a birdie two. As he plucks the ball from the hole, he turns and asks, "Hey, Travis, still glad to be paired with me?"

The bunker shot heard round the world, and the only one Tiger has had to hit the whole tournament, sets off another round of hysteria, and Seamus and I wait for things to calm down before we survey my putt. Would I like to answer his birdie with a birdie of my own? Sure, but I'm not that stupid. I don't think. I'm only eighteen feet from the hole but it's the wrong eighteen feet, all of them steeply downhill, and I'd be thrilled if I could stop it anywhere near the hole.

"Just breathe on it," says Seamus.

If only that were an option. Unfortunately, I have to hit it, and with the same piece of solid metal I just used to propel it 180 yards. How do I even begin to calculate the difference required? Should I try to tap it a billion times softer?

After some unseemly stalling, I touch the belly of the ball with the toe of my putter, intentionally hitting the ball off-center to lessen the impact. Seamus and I read in two inches of break from left to right but the ball is traveling too fast to take all of that and rolls over the left edge. It trickles past the hole by a foot, pauses, then trickles another foot, then picks up just enough speed to roll off the green and down the bank into the bunker that Tiger just vacated and my good buddy Steve Williams just raked.

Now I'm laying two in Strath, the bunker I hit putter off the tee to avoid. It's a bitter pill to swallow, like one of those enormous yellow multivitamins, but I remind myself I still have a substantial lead. The first priority is to get the ball safely out of the bunker and I do. But it carries ten feet too far, bounces off the back of the green and into a third bunker called Eden, which I saw no reason to mention until now. That was a mistake in story-telling as well as golf course management, because for the next ten minutes, without ever hitting an egregiously bad bunker shot, I ping-pong back and forth between Eden and Strath three times. When I finally get a chance to mark the ball again, I'm lying 10 and my entire lead has been squandered.

Not only that, I'm facing the identical eighteen feet for 11 that I was looking at nearly a half hour earlier for 2, although it now feels like a bygone era, a time to be recalled with nostalgia. The good old days.

"How can I possibly hit it any softer?" I ask Seamus.

"You can't," says Seamus. "We got to hole it."

This time, we split the difference and give it an inch and by an act of mercy—or pity—the ball bangs into the back of the hole and disappears. This doesn't set off an-other round of deafening applause. It's too late for that. Between Tiger's deuce and my *Spinal Tap*-ian 11, I have gone from eight in front to one behind.

54

THERE'S A BENCH OFF the 12th tee. I collapse onto it and for the second time today, take off my shoes and socks and dump out the sand. So much spills out, I think of those giant piles and earth-moving machinery by the hidden practice area.

"I'm not sure there's any sand left in those two bunkers," I say.

"Doesn't matter," says Seamus. "There's no one behind us."

"Good point."

Seamus seems neither deflated by the events on 11 nor put out by all that raking. "I know I told you this morning, and many times throughout the afternoon, that there was no way you were going to win this," says Seamus, "but I think I might have been wrong. Because that eighteen-footer you just rolled in was as brave a putt as

I've seen. You don't make that, we might still be back there."

"What was I going to do? Not hit it?"

"In any case, that's ancient history."

"Ancient?" I ask, looking back, literally and figuratively, at the 11th green, which is no more than thirty feet away. "You got to be kidding." Over Seamus's shoulder, I can make out Sarah and Noah desperately straining to get my attention, express their support, and make me feel a little better, Sarah with the reassurance in her smile and Noah with his tiny fist. But the wound is so fresh, I can barely face them.

"Travis, what you do on these next seven holes is your legacy. How you react could be the most valuable thing you leave your children. Are you going to curl into a fetal position after one bad hole? Okay, one very bad hole. Or are you going to set an example that could sustain and inspire your flesh and blood for generations?"

"That's a damn good question. Let me get back to you in a couple of days."

"We don't have a couple of days. And by the way, as a footnote, you're one shot out of the lead. With seven holes to play in the final round of the two hundredth playing of the Open Championship on the first and greatest course on the planet, you're alone in second, one stroke behind Tiger Woods. Forgive me if I'm speaking out of turn, but I suspect that if someone had offered you that at the start of the week, you might have been tempted to take it. So let's dump the last grains of Eden and Strath out of your FootJoys, lace them up, and go play some golf."

Although I refuse to give him the satisfaction of acknowledging it, Seamus's exhortation hits home. Everything he said is right and I know it. What I do on these next holes may not matter in the history of golf, but it does matter in the history of the McKinleys. It matters to Noah and Sarah and Elizabeth and will matter a shit ton to Simon, who has just set off on a similar treacherous path. And it matters to Dave and Ron and Chuck and my other friends back home. And it matters to me.

"Hey, Tiger," I say from the bench, "I think you got honors."

"I think you may be right," says Tiger with a more generous smile than he usually offers between the ropes. My quip was intended to send Tiger a message and also the gallery, but most of all, I said it for Sarah, to let her know that I'm all right, that it's just one frigging hole with some cruelly placed bunkering, and I'm not a broken shard of a human being whom she's going to have to spend the next thirty years cheering up. When I look over and smile at her, she's so relieved she's almost crying. By making Sarah and Noah feel better, I feel a lot better myself, and by the time I get up off the bench, the worst of my eleventh-hole hangover is gone.

My tee shot is a little shaky but I keep it left, and after an acceptable 7-iron and acceptable chip, I will my five-footer into the hole for one hell of a bounce-back par. Once that putt drops, I'm okay, and for the next four holes—13, 14, 15, and 16—I compete like hell. I match Tiger shot for shot, par for par, fist pump for fist pump, and when we reach 17, aka Road, the most famous hole in the sport, I'm still just one back.

55

SEVENTEEN IS AS HARD as cement. But the macadam pavement on Old Station Road that runs next to the green and gives the hole its name is only part of the problem. The hole is 466 yards and plays longer, and the tee shot is blind. As usual, out of bounds is right, but on 17 bailing left is not an option. Because the hole doglegs right, you have no choice but to start your tee shot in the direction of the trouble. In fact, you almost can't start it right enough, and your only chance of finding the fairway is to hit directly over the sheds of the Old Course Hotel, a surprisingly charmless edifice that runs along the right side of the fairway and that the McKinleys eschewed in favor of their much cozier motor home.

Tiger hasn't surrendered the honors since he seized them on No. 10 and tightens his grip with a perfect 3-wood straight over the sheds. Since I don't have his length or youth or anything else, I need to hit driver. Under pressure, I find that the smaller the target, the sharper the focus. If I'm aiming at a blade of grass, I'll pick one side of it. The name of the hotel is printed at the top of the shed and Seamus points and says "right over the *u* in *Course*," and I follow his instructions to the letter.

Even with driver, I'm 20 yards back of Tiger, 211 from the front edge.

For the most part, the Old Course greens are enormous, even after you divide the double greens in half, but 17 is the tiny amoeba-shaped anomaly, the smallest green on the course. Eating into the back-left side is another nasty high-banked bunker also called Road, and directly to the right, down a very short slope, the road itself, and every bit of it is in play. In keeping with tradition, the Sunday pin placement is at the back of the narrow green.

"The only sensible play," says Seamus, "is short to take the bunker and road out of the equation. But with one down and two to play, sensible isn't going to cut it."

"So what do you think?"

"Five-wood. It can't be over fifty degrees right now and to get to that back pin you're going to need all of it."

"Seamus, it's amazing how things work, isn't it?"

"How so?"

"One morning, just to feel like a human being, I get up early and go hit a bucket on a scruffy range in Encino, and now we're on the seventeenth fairway of Road, the mother of all golf holes on the mother of all golf courses. And that guy over there in the red shirt with that prick of a caddy beside him is Tiger Woods. How did this happen?"

"Travis, I suggest we set aside these bigger, broader questions for now and think about your next shot."

"My point is it comes down to people. The people who change your life. In this case, it came down to meeting you. Don't think I don't know that. Because I do. And I'm grateful."

"I appreciate that, Travis. Truly. And I'd appreciate it even more if you'd think about this five-wood, because not only is it the wrong shot for this hole, it's the hardest shot you've ever had to hit, and it's going to require every bit of focus you can muster and then some."

"Got it. Enough said."

56

I come close to hitting the 5-wood of my and Seamus's dreams. Excruciatingly close. I crawl into the quiet spot he urged me to find before every shot and the swing I put on it embodies everything about my game that is worthwhile. I flush it and the ball climbs into the cold damp air and banks left in a tight almost Tiger-esque draw. It bounces fifteen feet onto the green and rolls toward the back flag, but along the way it drifts ever so slightly right. That's all it takes to roll off the side and slip through the short fringe. When the ball finally stops, it sits precariously in the middle of the road like a disoriented turtle.

"That is *exactly* why the correct play was short in front," says Seamus, "but we got lucky."

Seeing me in the road gives Tiger all the more reason to hit the short percentage shot, but perhaps he is tired of me clinging to his pant leg and wants to settle this thing now, because he flights his 8-iron right at the hole. His swoosh-festooned ball travels an eerily similar arc to mine, and also rolls over the edge, through the fringe, and onto the road. The only difference is that Tiger's ball carries enough pace to roll through the road and comes to rest on a strip of grass between the macadam and a wall.

Our distances from the hole are close enough that the official with our group pulls out a tape measure, and while he determines who is away, Seamus and I take a good look at Tiger's lie. You'd think Tiger reaching the grass and us in the road would put us at a disadvantage, but it's the opposite. Chipping off macadam is hard for the club, not the golfer. The ball sits high, and knowing it's impossible to hit it fat removes most of the guesswork. After the official concludes that I'm far, I chip it cleanly and the ball skids to a stop, three feet from the hole.

A handful of players who've already completed their rounds have walked back from the clubhouse to watch these last couple of holes in person. Among them are Colin Montgomerie, Tom Lehman, Tiger's friend Notah Begay, and the Swedish star Jesper Parnevik. Parnevik is accompanied by his wife and children, the youngest of whom is carried by his blond nanny. Perhaps Tiger is human after all, because as the gallery backs away to give him room, he smiles flirtatiously at the striking young woman.

But what happens next is even more unlikely. Tiger's ball has come to rest on a strip of grass between the road and a wall about six feet short of a fire hydrant painted the same municipal yellow as the boot affixed to my rear tire, and although the hydrant is not close enough to impede his swing or pose a threat, Tiger stares at it intensely as if hypnotized. It's hard to fathom. Who other than Louie would be mesmerized by a fire hydrant, and maybe I'm imagining it, but when he finally turns away he seems shaken. In any case, he doesn't evince his usual razor-sharp focus and his pitch runs ten feet past the hole. When he leaves his comeback short and I clean up my three-footer, Tiger and I are tied for the lead.

57

I GUESS BY THE time this book comes out, you will already know what happened on 18, but for those who have more important things to reflect on than who sunk which putt when, let me refresh your memory.

Eighteen is the easiest driving hole on the course, sharing the same double 130-yard fairway as No. 1, and you don't have to worry about your ball trickling into the Swilcan Burn. On the other hand, no finishing hole is framed with as much history, geography, and architecture. The lack of a single tree makes the stone edifice of the R&A clubhouse even more imposing and has a similar effect on the sky and the sea. Running up the whole right flank of the hole is the town, and as you stand on the last tee you feel as if the entire population as well as the gray stone buildings themselves are welcoming you home. Add the minor detail that I'm tied with Tiger for the lead of the Open Championship, and that's a lot of gravitas for a former journeyman from the Senior Tour.

At 356 yards, I can't drive the hole, so Seamus sees little profit in trying. He'd rather see me hit a full wedge into the green than have to finesse something smaller. For the last time this week, Seamus gives me a target—the clock on the clubhouse—hands me a club—a hybrid 3—and asks me to kindly put some smooth on it. When the ball stops rolling, a full wedge is exactly what I have left.

Now Tiger commands the tee and for the next several minutes he and Williams barely exchange a word. No one has ever played the game like Tiger Woods and no one has ever taken his sweet time like him either. The way Tiger stands stock-still, his arms crossed in front of his chest, he could be waiting for a train. Or the one after it. When all is said and done, that stillness may be the thing about Tiger I'll remember most.

Finally, Tiger utters one word I can't quite hear, and Williams pulls the stuffed animal head off his driver. His practice swings contain all the audacity of an elite athlete at the peak of his powers, and the depth of his turn and the ungodly club head speed make my back hurt. For a second, I wish I were twenty-four again, but when I look at Sarah and Noah, the feeling passes. When Tiger finally makes the swing that counts, he unleashes another order of violence and the ball hisses off the head and hot-tails it straight at the Martyrs' Monument, where Seamus and I nursed our coffees and our dreams. It bounces just short of the hollow in front of the green called the Valley of Sin, races through the putting surface, and stops on the steep bank just beyond the green.

Seamus and I are still shaking our heads over Tiger's tee shot when we get to my ball a hundred yards short of that. "Poor fella," I whisper. "A three-hundred-sixty-six-yard par four and he's between clubs." Even with Tiger on the bank, I got a pretty good idea I'm going to need a birdie and take dead aim with my wedge. It's got the right weight and line and when it stops I've got all I could ask for—an uphill ten-footer for birdie.

The way Tiger's ball has settled in the rough, he can't do anything but trundle it down the hill. When it stops he's at least five feet farther from the hole than me and looking at a far trickier sidehill putt, but if Tiger is annoyed at the inequity of that, he doesn't show it. By now you probably remember what happened, but the amazing thing about witnessing it close up isn't the quality of Tiger's stroke or his read but how hard he hits it. He raps it so firm it takes all the break out of it and it might as well not be a sidehill putt at all and goes in dead center. If it hadn't, it would have lipped out or gone twenty feet past easy. But I guess that doesn't matter if you have no intention of missing.

Meanwhile, I still only have ten feet for the tie. Ten

feet uphill, exactly the kind of putt you want, and now it's Seamus's and my turn to take our sweet time and we look it over from every possible angle, including a few that have nothing to do with anything except trying to get my heart rate down. When he's reading it from behind the hole, Seamus even makes a little detour to whisper something to Sarah and Noah, before he comes back to me and says, "Just get it to the hole."

Despite all the reading/stalling, my heart rate is still way higher than ideal, but I don't have as much practice taking my time as Tiger, and I can't make myself wait any longer. I step up beside the putt, make two brisk practice strokes, take one last look, and let it go. My only thought is *Don't be short,* and it turns out that's not enough of a thought for someone who intends to win the Open Championship. I'm so determined not to leave it short, I yank it left and miss the cup by a foot, then walk over and tap in for a useless par.

After all that Sturm und Drang, it turns out Seamus was right all along.

There was no way anyone but Tiger Woods was going to win this tournament. In the end, Tiger was going to be Tiger and I was going to be Travis. But there is one thing Seamus was wrong about. As I'm standing there, agonizing over the fact that I just missed a ten-footer by a foot, Sarah and Noah and Louie come running out onto the green and throw themselves on me and Seamus with such unbridled affection and enthusiasm that the winner of the tournament has to fight through the celebration to shake the loser's hand.

"Great playing, Tiger," I say.

"You too, buddy. You almost gave Williams a heart attack."

58

THERE'S A LOT TO be said for establishing a routine in a foreign place. By now all four of us look forward with great anticipation to our little evening walk through town. Just because I missed a ten-footer by a foot is no reason not to enjoy it one last time.

When my responsibilities in the press tent are finally over and Seamus and the Mckinleys have exchanged email addresses and enjoyed one last fond embrace, we return to our favorite pub, where they've placed a RESERVED sign on an outside table and left a bowl of water under it for Louie. Then we follow our standard route past the shops and the movie house, Louie sniffing suspiciously at light poles and signposts to see who has been encroaching on his adopted terrain.

On all of our walks, we have felt the warmth of the residents, and tonight the whole town is sharing in our near victory, and on every block a local expresses congratulations and/or sympathies. "You gave us all a great thrill," says a woman about my age.

"And some hope," adds her companion. Mostly, though, they nod and smile and make us feel comfortable and at home.

We pass the enclosed courtyard of St. Salvator's College, which always makes me think of what it will be like when Noah heads off into the world, and then past the ruin of the cathedral and down to the water. As always, there's a bit of a line at the ice cream shack and we happily join it, refusing all offers to move us to the front of the queue. "This is one of our favorite parts of our visit," says Sarah, "and we're in no rush to see it end."

When it's our turn, we take our cones to the bench overlooking the tiny harbor, where the small boats are bobbing and creaking at their moorings. As we're enjoying our ice cream, a low-flying plane rips across the sky and we see the contrails of a private jet heading south along the ragged coast. "There goes Tiger," says someone at a nearby table, and I realize that overhead Tiger and his girlfriend and perhaps Williams and Nike CEO Phil Knight are toasting the latest Tiger triumph.

"He may have the Claret Jug and the private jet," I say, "but I hit the holy trifecta—best honey, great kid, loyal dog," and then the three of us touch cones instead of glasses.

"To St. Andrews," says Sarah, "and one hell of a trip."

"To my dad, who took it to eleven and still almost won the tournament," says Noah, and then he punctuates his toast by biting the head off his cone like Ozzy biting the head off a bat.

Tiger may be sipping champagne and I'm on a sticky bench overlooking a little harbor that smells of low tide, but I've never felt more grateful about my good fortune or more comfortable with my place in this world. Despite a couple of excruciating setbacks, a detour here and there, and a couple of three-putts of dubious quality, I haven't gone away. I'm still attempting something very hard. Still thinking to a large degree about the future. Still in the game. And how could you possibly ask for more than that?

When Sarah finishes her ice cream, we head back up the hill, passing the cathedral again, but this time from the back, and then turn onto the quiet little street that has been our home for the past four days. When we reach the St. Andrews School of Economics we step through the gate and walk to the parking lot in the rear. As always, the van is a welcome sight, and Louie tugs hard at his leash in anticipation of his comfortable circular bed. Alongside it, he stops pulling and sniffs warily.

"The van looks different," says Noah.

"You're right," says Sarah. "The 'trespassing' stickers on the windows have been peeled off and the yellow boot has been removed. And it's clean! Somebody washed it."

In place of the stickers is a light blue envelope and inside, a piece of stationery of the same color on which has been written a short note.

Dear McKinleys, it reads. *Please accept our apologies for any inconvenience. Stay as long as you like, and come back very soon. With highest regards and warmest affection, the residents of St. Andrews.*

ABOUT THE AUTHORS

JAMES PATTERSON is one of the best-known and biggest-selling writers of all time. His books have sold in excess of 385 million copies worldwide. He is the author of some of the most popular series of the past two decades – the Alex Cross, Women's Murder Club, Detective Michael Bennett and Private novels – and he has written many other number one bestsellers including romance novels and stand-alone thrillers.

James is passionate about encouraging children to read. Inspired by his own son who was a reluctant reader, he also writes a range of books for young readers including the Middle School, I Funny, Treasure Hunters, Dog Diaries and Max Einstein series. James has donated millions in grants to independent bookshops and has been the most borrowed author of adult fiction in UK libraries for the past eleven years in a row. He lives in Florida with his wife and son.

PETER DE JONGE is the author of the critically acclaimed crime novels *Shadows Still Remain* and *Buried on Avenue B*. Before collaborating on *Miracle at St Andrews*, he and James Patterson cowrote *Miracle on the 17th Green* and *Miracle at Augusta*.

To see more of Travis's story, pick up *Miracle at Augusta.*

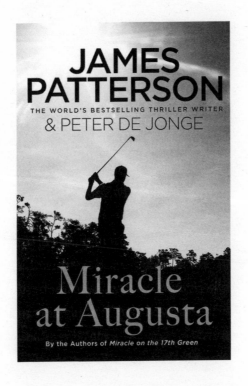

FOR AN EXCERPT, TURN THE PAGE.

1

"ON THE FIRST TEE...from Winnetka, Illinois...the 1996 winner of the U.S. Senior Open...Travis McKinley."

I've never set foot on Augusta National before, let alone teed it up, so for thirty seconds, I just stand there shivering and let the polite applause of the patrons wash over me. Okay, "wash over me" is a bit of a stretch. How about "trickle over me"? Could you live with that? While the clapping subsides, I close my eyes and picture the shot I need to hit.

Because my grandfather gave me a book on the Masters one Christmas, I happen to know that Augusta was originally a nursery owned by a Belgian horticulturist named Prosper Berckmans. That's why all the holes are named after trees. The first, Tea Olive, is a 445-yard par 4, which doglegs left and calls for a high fade to the right side of the fairway some 290 yards away. When the image of the shot is locked in my mind, I step up and launch my drive into the December gloom, aiming twenty feet right of the big wire net that keeps balls from flying into the parking lot of the CVS next door.

I'm happy to report that my tee shot comes off pretty much as planned, leaving me 165 yards to an uphill green, so I swap the driver for my 7-iron and aim for the right rear corner of it. When the ball lands softly and trickles—like that applause—toward the pin, tucked up front, just beyond the trap, I give myself the eight-footer for birdie and move on to the par-five 2nd, aka Pink Dogwood.

My body may be fifteen miles outside of Chicago, freezing its nearly fifty-two-year-old ass off at the Big Oaks Driving Range on Route 38, but in my mind it's in Georgia in April, and those color-corrected dogwoods and azaleas have old Prosper turning over in his grave.

The start of my third year on the Senior Tour is a month away. As some of you may recall, my rookie year went rather well—unkind sportswriters leaned heavily on the word *miraculous*—culminating in my win at Pebble, which the starter was gracious enough to mention. My sophomore season, however, was lackluster at best, so I'm doing everything I can to prepare for '98, particularly since the shelf life out here is so brief, what with me growing more decrepit by the day and fresh young blood bubbling up from below. If you think it's hard fighting for scraps left by Hale Irwin, Gil Morgan, and Hank Peters, and believe me it is, imagine what it will be like next year when Tom Watson, Lanny Wadkins, and Tom Kite flash their birth certificates and step up to the senior buffet.

I don't even want to think about that. I just know that this year is huge, and since the end of October, I've been at Big Oaks every afternoon, fifth stall from the left, chewing up these nasty rubber mats and whatever cartilage is left in my right elbow.

To relieve the tedium, I've been playing virtual rounds at Augusta, hole by hole, Flowering Crab Apple to Carolina Cherry, seeing if I can find the correct half of the fairway and then land it on the correct quadrant of the green. Along the way, I try to keep my scuffed range rock from rolling back into Rae's Creek or finding the pine straw or nestling up behind the Eisenhower tree. It keeps me sharper than mindlessly banging balls.

For the front side, the nine they never put on the air, I make do with the pictures and descriptions in my old Christmas present, but for the back nine, I have thirty years of TV viewing to draw on. When I get to 12, Golden Bell, that nasty par 3 at the end of Amen Corner, I even know which tree Byron Nelson used to look at to decipher the swirling winds. Instead, I gaze roofward and see if there are any plastic bags whipping around in the currents. My favorite holes are 13 and 15, Azalea and Firethorn, the two short par 5s that have been the scene of so much drama. In the last couple of weeks, I've even been working on a high draw to keep it on those slippery greens, which, in my mind at least, are never less than 13.2 on the Stimpmeter.

Today, at 15, I catch it solid off the tee, and since I get even more roll off the Big Oaks cement than I would from the hard, sloping fairways at Augusta, I've only got 215 left, a perfect yardage for my new pet draw. As I prepare to launch the ball into the azure sky, there's a bang behind my left shoulder. It sounds like a shotgun blast but is in fact a shank from Esther Lee, the housewife in the stall to my left.

"Sorry about that," says Esther, raising a hand in a pink glove.

"No problem," I reply. But the reverie is broken, and suddenly it's a lot harder to pretend I'm in Georgia and not a drafty warehouse in suburban Chicago. After a couple more swings, I pack it in for the day and deposit my bag in the closet behind the front desk, where the manager has been nice enough to let me keep it, seeing as I'm here five days a week.

Then I drive the nine miles to Winnetka and get in line with all the other trophy housewives and husbands and wait for Noah to be released from his kindergarten classroom at Belltown Grammar. Elizabeth and Simon were already well grown when Noah made a surprise appearance nearly six years ago, and as I watch the little gink shuffle out of the back, his backpack hanging off one shoulder and his baseball cap turned backwards, I appreciate how lucky Sarah and I are.

"Hey, Noah, how was your day?"

"Not bad. How about you? How was Augusta?"

"Shot thirty-two on the front."

"Give yourself a lot of eight-footers?"

"You know what I say, Noah?"

"Charity begins at home."

"Exactly."

Our house is less than five minutes from the school, and seeing Sarah's Cherokee in the driveway makes us both uneasy.

"Mom's home early."

"Yeah."

When we get out of the car, Sarah is standing in the doorway. "I have some sad news to share," she tells us. "Pop died."

2

AT 2 P.M. THE FOLLOWING Saturday, some two hundred of my grandfather's friends convene in the parking lot of the Creekview Country Club and follow him up the frozen first fairway. By now, Pop has been reduced to the ashes that fill the Tupperware container head pro Matt Higgins holds in the crook of his left arm. When Higgins reaches the first green, he pulls off one glove, pries open the lid, and sprinkles a bit of Edwin Joseph McKinley over the portion of the green where the hole is generally cut.

As the gray soot rains down on the winter green, Higgins utters the signature words with which my grandfather started a thousand rounds: "No gimmes. No mulligans. No bullshit. Let's play golf," and the ragtag army, some of whom have been forced by age and infirmity to ride golf carts with home health aides, hurl it back in unison like a battle cry: "No gimmes! No mulligans! No bullshit! Let's play golf!" Then Higgins hands Pop off like a football, and another volunteer takes the lead.

It's an impressive turnout, particularly considering it's fourteen degrees. Included in the boisterous band of mourners is my best friend and former caddy, Earl Fielder, who came up last night from North Carolina. No doubt my grandfather would be touched to see so many dear friends. Pop, who hated slow play, would also appreciate the brisk pace. In forty minutes, the procession covers thirteen holes, and with five left, the next two generations of McKinleys take over.

Simon, a freshman at Northwestern, leads us up the par-five 14th. He carries his grandfather over the longest hole on the course, then turns him over to his proud younger brother, and now the chilled brigade, many of whom have been fortifying themselves with frequent nips from their pocket flasks, fall in line behind a five-year-old. After Noah guides them to the 15th green, they take particular delight in the unlikely spectacle of a kindergartner leading them through another chorus of "No gimmes! No mulligans! No bullshit! Let's play golf!"

But it's the McKinley ladies, Elizabeth and Sarah, who get to me the most on this freezing afternoon. Elizabeth, because she is surely the most devastatingly beautiful radiology resident in North America, and Sarah...because she's Sarah. Sarah walks off 17, she hands off Pop with a kiss, and it's up to me to carry him home.

Affection for my grandfather is inscribed on every face in this unholy procession, many of whom are by now overfortified, but for me the affection and appreciation are overwhelming. Without my grandfather, I have no idea where, or even who, I'd be. I wouldn't be a golfer. When I was eight, he put a cut-down 7-iron in my hand, and for the last forty-three years or so he's been my only coach. And when Leo Burnett tossed me to the curb a couple of Christmases ago, he was the only one who didn't think my grandiose scheme of qualifying for the Senior Tour was insane. I've been so dependent on his guidance, on and off the course, for so long, I'm more than a little worried how I'll do without it.

I carry Pop the final third of a mile and sprinkle what's left on 18, banging the bottom of the container like a bongo to make sure every last particle of the beloved man has been set free.

"No gimmes! No mulligans! No bullshit!" I shout. "Let's have a drink!"

"I think he means an indoor drink," says an old friend, turning over an empty flask, and we file into the clubhouse for one last round or three on Edwin Joseph McKinley.

3

AFTER EARL HAS RUN a gauntlet of McKinley hugs and kisses and accepted pats on the back and best wishes from a dozen of my grandfather's starstruck old cronies, I walk my friend from the clubhouse into the freezing Midwestern night. At the end of the flagstone path, a cab is waiting to take him to the airport, and as we approach the car, I realize, and not for the first time, that I also owe a great debt to Earl, without whom I never could have succeeded in my rookie year, and although I feel the urge to finally thank him in clear and explicit English, I fall short, in the finest male tradition.

"Thanks again for making the trip" is about the best I can manage. "As you can see, it meant a lot to all of us."

"It meant a lot to me too, Travis. When you kick off, I'll come to yours, too."

"Promise?"

"Yup."

"Thanks."

"See you in a couple of weeks, then. You ready?"

"I better be. I've been working my ass off."

"Good. Because I don't want to embarrass you out there."

When we've exchanged as much of this as we can stomach, Earl gets into the car, and I walk to the back of the lot and get into mine. After letting the heat run for five minutes, I pull up in front, where Sarah, Elizabeth, Simon, and Noah pile in.

Creekview Country Club is an older course and, like a lot of older courses, is in the center of a neighborhood that has deteriorated over the decades. On the way back to the highway we pass a series of strip malls, lined with liquor stores, pawnshops, and mini-marts that seem particularly threadbare on such a raw night.

In the last year and a half, I've done pretty well, almost embarrassingly so, and my one indulgence has been this Mercedes sedan. Although I've had it six months, I often still feel uncomfortable behind the wheel, an impostor, but the one time I never regret the purchase is on a night like this, when it's stuffed with McKinleys and I feel that, at least for the duration of the trip, the tanklike vehicle is protecting them all, not just from the wind and cold but from all life's other harsh realities as well.

Plus, as Noah often points out, it's kind of swank.

Up ahead, at the light, a broken-down old van sits on the side of the road. As I wait for the light to turn, a middle-aged woman climbs out of the driver's seat to gauge the extent of her problem, and when she walks in front of her car, we make eye contact. I know I should pull over, but the lateness of the hour and the sketchiness of the neighborhood lobby against it, and before I can offer a convincing counterargument, the light turns green and the impregnable Benz rolls on.

Two stoplights later, my conscience gets the better of me, or maybe I just feel the heat of Elizabeth's gaze on the back of my neck. "I'm going to circle back," I say, more to myself than anyone else. "See if I can help her."

It's a four-lane road and half a mile before I can make a U-turn. By the time I get back to the woman and her van, I'm relieved to see that a second just as beat-up car has pulled over and parked behind it, and an older man, African-American with a gray beard, is wrestling a spare tire onto the right rear wheel. I roll down the window and the cold air rushes in.

"Need any help?"

"That's okay," says the man, taking in the well-dressed family from below.

"Sure?"

"It's just a flat tire, sport. We got it covered."

4

IF THERE'S A BETTER place to spend mid-January than Hawaii, let me know. Till then I'll have to make do with Waialae Country Club on the island of Oahu, where Earl and I are getting our last reps in before tomorrow's start of the Azawa Open and warming our bones in the tropical sun. It feels so good to be warm, and out of that stall at Big Oaks, I'm hardly bothered by the fact that fifty people are lined up on the range behind Earl, and two are watching me, one of whom is my new caddy, Johnny Abate. Earl's fans, who have taken to calling themselves Earl's Platoon, aren't content to stand and gape. Every time he pures another 4-iron, they ooh and ahh and shower him with love.

"This is your year, Earl!"

"Hell yeah, buddy."

"You're the man, EF!"

And my personal favorite—"Earl Fielder is EFing good."

"I guess they don't get out much," I mumble under my breath to the object of all this adulation.

"What makes you say that, Travis?"

To clarify, I should probably point out that Earl has enjoyed a dramatic change in fortune since caddying for me in my rookie season in '96. For starters, he is now a member of the Senior Tour himself. He earned his playing privileges by finishing second in the '97 Senior Q-School, then backed it up with one of the most consistent rookie seasons ever, ending the year with twenty-three straight top tens. But what changed everything and transformed him into a bona fide celebrity is that Reebok commercial, which juxtaposes Earl on tour with old footage and photos of him from the late sixties in Vietnam. No one is happier for Earl than me, but do I find the clamor for autographs and photographs at restaurants and airports just a wee bit annoying?

Of course not. I'm a bigger person than that.

"Work on anything in the off-season?" I ask.

"Just tried to tighten everything up a notch. Keep the arms and body more attached, have it all move in one piece."

"Jesus, Earl. You already got the most buttoned-up swing out here. To get it any tighter you'd need a monkey wrench." But as Earl stripes a couple more, I realize he may actually have succeeded. Watching Earl, his broad forehead beaded with sweat, is like watching an Old World Italian mason build a wall. There's no wasted motion. Every move and gesture is pared to the nub.

"You're striping it better than ever, Earl, and that's saying something. You're going to get that win this year, maybe two."

"I wouldn't bet on it," says Earl. "I'm too much of a grinder. I may not stink it up, but I rarely go real low, either. Don't roll it well enough. But I'd trade all those seconds and thirds for one win. And not just for the exemption. I want something to be remembered for, and once you get your name engraved on silver, it's hard to get it off. How about you, Trav? You work on anything up there on the tundra?"

"See for yourself."

I pull my 5-wood, aim my club face and feet slightly right of my target, and as I swing, I focus on keeping my hips turning and really letting my arms go, ripping down, through, and up. The ball takes off with the usual trajectory but, a hundred yards out, shoots up like a rocket when the afterburners hit. It bends slightly to the left before landing softly 215 yards away.

"Son of a bitch," says Earl. "I need to see you do that again."

I dislodge another Titleist from the pyramid-shaped pile, nudge it into place beside the long, shallow divot, and turn on the ball one more time.

"Well, I'll be damned. The high fucking draw. The suavest shot in golf. I just have one question."

"What's that?"

"Why? There isn't one hole out here where you'll need it."

"It's for Augusta."

"Augusta?"

"How else am I going to keep the ball on those reachable par fives, thirteen and fifteen in particular? Those are birdie holes, Earl. You're not birdieing those, you're losing half a stroke to the field."

"I know that, Travis. You're not the only one with a TV."

"You get reception down there?"

"How the hell are you going to get an invitation—steal it from Tiger's mailbox?"

"Haven't thought that far ahead. You know it's a mistake to get ahead of yourself in this game. I just have a feeling I'm going to need it."

5

THE DISPARITY IN STATUS between Earl and me is reflected in our Friday tee times. Earl goes off in the early afternoon with Chi Chi Rodriguez and Raymond Floyd, and I slip out at 7:03 a.m. with senior rookies Trent Smith and Elliot Brody. I hadn't heard of them either, until I looked them up in the media guide. Smith joined the navy out of high school. Back on dry land, he sold insurance, ran a nightclub, and repaired pin-setting machines at a bowling alley, then spent fifteen years in Grand Prairie, Texas, in the auto repair business. He got into the field by Monday qualifying. Brody, who earned his spot through this year's Q-School, was a teaching pro outside Tacoma for thirty years.

It couldn't be a more congenial group. One look at each other and we knew we were all just slightly different versions of the same person—three guys who hadn't seriously considered making a living at competitive golf till it was almost too late, and now we're determined to make the most of our chance. What little chatter there is, is collegial and supportive, each of us giving the others the chance to do their best.

The setting isn't half bad, either. With no one in front of us, I feel like I washed ashore in paradise and just happened to find my sticks here waiting for me. The only sounds are waves, rustling palms, and birds. If anyone had gotten up at dawn and wandered over, they would have seen some quality golf. Among the three of us, we carded one bogey and fourteen birdies. All those sessions at Big Oaks must have paid off, or maybe it's the novel thrill of hitting off organic material, because six of those birdies are mine. For the next four hours, my 66 makes me the year's top player on the Senior Tour, and when the last player walks off 18, I'm tied for second with Gil Morgan, one shot behind the leader, Hale Irwin.

6

FRIDAY, I WENT OFF in the first group of the day. On Saturday, thanks to that 66, I go off in the final one. Instead of playing under the radar with two fellow journeymen, I'm trading shots with the two best fifty-somethings on the planet—Hale Irwin and Gil Morgan. Last year, Irwin won nine tournaments and more money than any golfer in the world, including an elegant young cat named Tiger Woods. Morgan won six times and earned more than Tiger, too. The last time I felt this out of my league was the summer afternoon in college when I got it into my head to play pickup basketball at a playground on the South Side of Chicago.

Everyone knows about Irwin, the former all–Big Eight cornerback with three U.S. Open titles, but it's the late-blooming Morgan who is the revelation. For one thing, he possesses a perfect swing. Literally. When he was a kid, his father, a small-town mortician, took him to see Harvey Penick, the legendary Austin pro who taught Ben Crenshaw and Tom Kite. Penick took one look at Morgan's move and sent him home. Said there was nothing he could do for him.

Irwin's swing is not nearly as lovely and he's much shorter off the tee, but he possesses a level of competitiveness and confidence that is borderline psychotic. As impressed as I am that Morgan hits it twenty yards past Irwin all day, I'm even more impressed by the fact that Irwin could truly not care less.

I don't want to belabor the point, but here's one last illustration of the chasm in golfing prowess between me and them. Last year Irwin led the tour with an average score of 68.93, and my average was a shade under 71. In other words, if we had a regular game at Creekview Country Club on Sunday mornings, he would have to give me a stroke a side. But at Waialae on Saturday afternoon, I didn't need any strokes from anyone. When our round is in the books, I've carded my second straight 66 to Irwin's 69 and Morgan's 70.

Those aren't typos. That's just golf.

Also by James Patterson

ALEX CROSS NOVELS

Along Came a Spider • Kiss the Girls • Jack and Jill •
Cat and Mouse • Pop Goes the Weasel • Roses are Red •
Violets are Blue • Four Blind Mice • The Big Bad Wolf •
London Bridges • Mary, Mary • Cross • Double Cross •
Cross Country • Alex Cross's Trial (*with Richard DiLallo*) •
I, Alex Cross • Cross Fire • Kill Alex Cross • Merry
Christmas, Alex Cross • Alex Cross, Run • Cross My
Heart • Hope to Die • Cross Justice • Cross the Line •
The People vs. Alex Cross • Target: Alex Cross

STAND-ALONE THRILLERS

The Thomas Berryman Number • Hide and Seek • Black
Market • The Midnight Club • Sail (*with Howard Roughan*) •
Swimsuit (*with Maxine Paetro*) • Don't Blink (*with Howard
Roughan*) • Postcard Killers (*with Liza Marklund*) • Toys (*with
Neil McMahon*) • Now You See Her (*with Michael Ledwidge*) • Kill
Me If You Can (*with Marshall Karp*) • Guilty Wives (*with David
Ellis*) • Zoo (*with Michael Ledwidge*) • Second Honeymoon (*with
Howard Roughan*) • Mistress (*with David Ellis*) • Invisible (*with
David Ellis*) • Truth or Die (*with Howard Roughan*) • Murder
House (*with David Ellis*) • Woman of God (*with Maxine Paetro*) •
Humans, Bow Down (*with Emily Raymond*) • The Black Book (*with
David Ellis*) • Murder Games (*with Howard Roughan*) • The Store
(*with Richard DiLallo*) • Texas Ranger (*with Andrew Bourelle*) •
The President is Missing (*with Bill Clinton*) • Revenge
(*with Andrew Holmes*) • Juror No. 3 (*with Nancy Allen*) •
The First Lady (*with Brendan DuBois*)

DETECTIVE MICHAEL BENNETT SERIES

Step on a Crack (*with Michael Ledwidge*) • Run for Your Life
(*with Michael Ledwidge*) • Worst Case (*with Michael Ledwidge*) •
Tick Tock (*with Michael Ledwidge*) • I, Michael Bennett
(*with Michael Ledwidge*) • Gone (*with Michael Ledwidge*) •
Burn (*with Michael Ledwidge*) • Alert (*with Michael Ledwidge*) •
Bullseye (*with Michael Ledwidge*) • Haunted (*with James O. Born*) •
Ambush (*with James O. Born*)

PRIVATE NOVELS

Private (*with Maxine Paetro*) • Private London (*with Mark Pearson*) • Private Games (*with Mark Sullivan*) • Private: No. 1 Suspect (*with Maxine Paetro*) • Private Berlin (*with Mark Sullivan*) • Private Down Under (*with Michael White*) • Private L.A. (*with Mark Sullivan*) • Private India (*with Ashwin Sanghi*) • Private Vegas (*with Maxine Paetro*) • Private Sydney (*with Kathryn Fox*) • Private Paris (*with Mark Sullivan*) • The Games (*with Mark Sullivan*) • Private Delhi (*with Ashwin Sanghi*) • Private Princess (*with Rees Jones*)

NYPD RED SERIES

NYPD Red (*with Marshall Karp*) • NYPD Red 2 (*with Marshall Karp*) • NYPD Red 3 (*with Marshall Karp*) • NYPD Red 4 (*with Marshall Karp*) • NYPD Red 5 (*with Marshall Karp*)

DETECTIVE HARRIET BLUE SERIES

Never Never (*with Candice Fox*) • Fifty Fifty (*with Candice Fox*) • Liar Liar (*with Candice Fox*)

NON-FICTION

Torn Apart (*with Hal and Cory Friedman*) • The Murder of King Tut (*with Martin Dugard*) • All-American Murder (*with Alex Abramovich and Mike Harvkey*)

MURDER IS FOREVER TRUE CRIME

Murder, Interrupted (*with Alex Abramovich and Christopher Charles*) • Home Sweet Murder (*with Andrew Bourelle and Scott Slaven*) • Murder Beyond the Grave (*with Andrew Bourelle and Christopher Charles*)

For more information about James Patterson's novels, visit
www.jamespatterson.co.uk